THE CELL BLOCK PRESENTS...

COCAINE QUEEN

BOOK ONE

Published by: The Cell Block™

The Cell Block
P.O. Box 1025
Rancho Cordova, CA 95741

Website: thecellblock.net
Facebook/thecellblockofficial
Instagram: @mikeenemigo
Corrlinks: info@thecellblock.net

Cover Design: Mike Enemigo

Send comments, reviews, interview and business inquiries to: info@thecellblock.net

PART 1
THE KILLING OF A BOY
ALEJANDRO

CHAPTER 1

1) 1974

Bed springs squeaked loudly in rhythm with the moaning. It was a sound Griselda knew well and had gotten used to over the years. The dilapidated shack they called home seemed to work as an echo chamber for just the occasion. Something she'd learn later that her mother took advantage of by really making the guys feel like they were getting the job done. This was mom's work time, Griselda knew, as she listened through the closet door. Ana relied on the closet as a sort of babysitter for Griselda since they moved into the shack.

Griselda didn't like it very much.

There was the smell of wet wood. There was the fact that creepy crawlies would occasionally find their way into the closet. Once a rat ran across her legs and she came screaming out of the closet to her mother's chagrin and the man's mortification, as he jumped from the bed, his hand covering his privates, while she ran into the naked arms of her mother.

Hearing her mother moan along with the man she brought home, Griselda tried to tune it out, humming gently to herself. It was a hot night. Most nights in Columbia were hot, especially in Medellin, but tonight felt especially so. Sweat soaked the front of her shirt and dust and grime matted to her skin.

1

Laying there, knowing that somewhere, she had family, a grandmother and grandfather out in the world, she wondered what would have happened if her mother never left Cartagena, if her father never ran out on her and her mother when she was born, what their life would be like now. There were thoughts about feeling her father's warm hugs. She always imagined him as a warm and loving man, even though he ran out on them. There were thoughts of hugs and kisses, powerful embraces that made her feel safe, and a feeling that her life could be good.

They would live in an actual house. Not a ghetto shack. But an actual house, like the people did just a mile down the road from her neighborhood. She thought better… because it was hard to imagine that it could be worse. She was sure "better" was the right word.

She would try sometimes to remember Cartagena. The port city that was on the Northern coast of Colombia. It had bustling boats and the smell of ocean breeze, better than the sweaty, mildewy wood and rusty metal that surrounded everything that was her life. There was a stink to the slums. A lack of hygiene, only one of the sharp scents. The rot, the rust, the mold, it all had its own smell and own flavor. A sense that tingled the tongue. If you had your wits about you, there was money to be made there. The bustling port city that she was born in, that she spent the first three years of her life at, that there was family there that she hadn't visited in three or four years and probably never would visit again.

Sitting in the closet, she just continued to try to distract herself. Usually escaping into her imagination.

Thinking of her life as a Princess taken from her kingdom and forced into a life as a pauper. Imagining the day when she would return to her empire and be crowned a queen. Rich and powerful. Living in mansions. Having people wait on her. Everything, everything… EVERYTHING would be clean!

Then the moldy smell from the wet wood tickled her small nose and the sounds of her mother brought her back to the reality and saddened her. The thin wood panel that separated her from the earth below shifted about whenever she adjusted her body. Her mother moaned once more. The soft guttural groan of false pleasure, followed by the man moaning along with her. It was coming to an end, Griselda knew, and it always got louder when that happened, so Griselda put her hands over her ears and hummed softly to herself – knowing no one would notice.

When Griselda's mother put her in the closet for the first time, it freaked her out, and she rolled herself into a ball and cried for the six hours her mother left her in there. Her mother had moved a bureau in front of the door that kept her stuck in there no matter how much she tried to open the door. The next dozen times she kept locking her in, until Griselda finally stopped trying to open the door, or fight Ana when she wanted her to go in, and eventually, her mother stopped locking her in.

She cried frequently each day, or at least the first few dozen times she was in there. She couldn't stop herself. Then, eventually, like anything, it just became normal. And it was something that she'd remember later in life. Anything could become normal if you do it enough. Anything. And after that she went into the closet and sat quietly, twirling her hair, playing with anything she could find, usually the hems of coats and dresses her mother had, and just waiting until her mother was finished, or until sleep took her. Just thinking to herself. Thinking about life as different.

Griselda preferred to sit, her back against the wall, hidden behind the small dresses and jackets, draped shakingly over a large poll above head. Griselda balled one up as a pillow, leaning herself against the cool wood, and continued to listen. Those springs singing along with every joyful grunt and all Griselda could think was that she couldn't wait until she figured her way out of this place.

There weren't many that did. She was aware of that.

Julio Brava, an old man, who's right hand he held to his chest, to keep its arthritic deformity from prying eyes, and sold fruits and meats from a cart, had been in Medellin, in the poor, impoverished slum that Griselda lived, his entire life. In fact, most of the poor and struggling had been here their entire lives. From Stella Boso, who worked the streets like her mother, to her friends Rafi, whose parents who lived in a shack smaller than hers and had two sisters with him.

Here in Medellin, in the slums, people lived stacked on top of each other, with tin roofs that sounded like gunfire when it rained hard enough, and leaked like a broken faucet onto the thin plywood floors.

Their shack felt especially vulnerable. With a mixture of desiccated wood, red brick, and aluminum paneling on the sides, the same as the roof, rain poured in like they barely had a roof. The floor was made of large flat pieces of plywood, in which several pieces had cracked, or broken, and dirt had begun to show between the cracks and with grass growing between those cracks.

The squeaking springs got quicker and the man's grunts turned louder, more excited, until he howled like a hound, and everything went still. This was the usual pattern for Ana Blanco's male guests. She brought them home after going out and leaving Griselda alone. She'd come in, high or drunk, and push Griselda into the closet. Then she'd fuck the man she brought home. Occasionally she'd go out again and bring another home. And occasionally she wouldn't come home at all. Griselda hated her mother. Hated the way her mother treated her. Hated the way her mother let other people treat her. And as the silence filled the small closet, and the springs shivered and quaked as people got off of it, she hated that this was her life.

2)

The streets bustled during the day, just as much as they did at night. All that was different was how everything moved. At night, the slums of Medellin filled with prostitutes, drug dealers, and a host of elements looking to make a quick buck, or score what they have enough money for and get back to their shanty. There was a chaos, a beautiful, dangerous chaos to it, that ebbed and flowed until the dawn, for which, like nocturnal animals, people slid back into hiding until the sunset once more. During the day, there were storefronts and signs, people calling out services, and carts brimming with meats and vegetables and fruits.

There was the smell of cooking in the air, sizzling fat, eggs, and grease.

People shouted from their carts, trying to tout the freshness of their food. Chickens were in cages, clucking away, flapping their wings and balking as they got jostled by the seller, while he proclaimed, "I'll kill it and pack it for you right here." Griselda loved to eat. She loved food. Possibly because of the many days that she'd go without it sometimes. The seller kept hollering, "A great meal, great meal!"

The shops were decorative, often with walls of colored clay, and simple windows. They lined the main streets with them. Each store served the community well, selling clothes and cigarettes and a host of basic things that for Griselda was a great place to steal from. She didn't remember the first thing she ever stole, since she had been doing it since before, she really had memories. If she had to choose a year, she probably would say around age five, though she wouldn't have put it past herself to have grabbed stuff as an infant.

There was a pleasure to it. A joy at getting something for nothing. A pleasure in knowing that she could get for herself, even at a young age. It felt good to have some fresh fruit, some candy, and other food when she wanted it. It felt good to not rely on her mother, not that Griselda ever could rely on her.

For Griselda, as she'd spent her days walking around Medellin and leaving her mother alone to sleep all day, Medellin was bothersome to her. As much as it was beautiful, as much as it was home. From her abject poverty, to the wealthy and powerful, in just a couple of miles of walking. The wealthy in Medellin had large houses, with gorgeous yards, and a smell of freshness in the air that was tamped by food, sweat, and dyes.

Of course, she could never stay in those neighborhoods long. The police patrolled those streets well and shunned any of the "undesirables" from those neighborhoods. And Griselda was well aware that she was one of those undesirables. They would yell at her to go home. To get off the streets. That if they caught her stealing, they would put her in prison. And they scared her. Scared her enough that she never stole from the wealthy side of town. Not that they let her into those types of stores in the first place. They scared her enough that she resented the people of wealth and prosperity as much as she envied them.

She and her small group of older friends liked to go into those communities for a little fun though, get stared at by people, and some of her friends were brazen enough to run in and steal, and they'd run home, sandals clacking along the way while they laughed. Her friends made her life worth living. Street kids like herself, each and every one of them, with stories like her own. They let her smoke pot with them. At first, she's sure, they probably just wanted to see what would happen if they got a ten-year-old high. But all that happened was that she giggled dumbly, stared off into space, and asked them if they had anything to eat, because she was starving.

There was Rafi. He was cute. So cute. The oldest of the group.

She liked to steal hair gel for him, because she thought he looked like Bogart, just darker and younger, when he had his hair slick back.

Lydia was his sister, a year younger at fourteen. She was kind of like the mother of the group. She asked if anyone was hungry; she planned out things for them to do, and she vetoed her brother's more stupid ideas. Magenta, Maggie, was the one who brought her into the group. She was six months older than Griselda, and the first time they met, they hit it off immediately when Maggie stole an apple for Griselda. It was a rare act of kindness that Griselda rarely encountered.

They had a few other friends in the group. Markos, whose family used to have money until his father got killed. Jacko, who was a twitchy fourteen-year-old who loved weed about as much as a person could love a plant. If it had a hole, he'd fuck it. And Yessica, Lydia's best friend, who spent most of her time trying to get Rafi to notice her.

Today, on a rather hot day in June, things felt different when she met up with the crew. Their usual hang out place was a ratty desolate field behind the shops, where people left old rotted cars, and tossed out junk they didn't want, or couldn't use, turning it into a swampy, rotting dump of metal and fabric and plastic that had its fair share of scavengers. They weren't some of them. It was just the best place to not be bothered. Anyone that was there didn't care what the hell a group of kids were doing there.

"We need to make some fucking money and we need to make it fucking now," said Lydia.

"Porque?" Griselda asked, as she came in on the conversation in the middle.

"Mom wants Lydia out on the streets to help bring in more money," said Rafi. It was the sad but constant fate for a lot of the young women that were here, one that Griselda herself dreaded but suspected she wouldn't be spared from.

"I'm sorry."

"Don't be sorry. Just help us out," said Rafi, who was sitting on top of a burnt-up Renault, and he slid himself down and dusted off his hands. A brownish red mark stained his shirt around the shoulders and neck in a way that looked like blood. But most of his clothes had some stain on it. Rafi took Griselda's hands in his. If you could help Lydia, you would, wouldn't you?"

Griselda smiled and nodded. She liked the rough touch of his hands on hers. The way his dark brown eyes stared into hers. She wished she was older, as pretty as Lydia. But her face was roundish, and her hair thin and her mother kept cutting it in a bob when she cut it. Ana, ever the fashionista, would say how much this was like how the models were wearing their hair.

"We have a plan that could get us all a lot of money," he said.

"Even me?"

"Even you," said Lydia.

"We got Markos and Yessica already in place. Maggie and you don't have to do much, you're more the bait, and we'll take care of the rest. But unlike when you go fishing, the bait will not get eaten. Okay? No matter what. We wouldn't put Maggie or you in danger. You believe that right?"

She'd believe anything that Rafi told her. She bit her pink lip and nodded. "What do I have to do?" she asks.

Rafi and Lydia smiled.

3)

9

The Ribaldi's lived in a wealthy part of town. The father worked in import and exporting for American and Colombian companies, creating connections for products, and helping organize the distribution of goods to consumer outlets, while managing graft and corruption. They paid him very well for it. He was, by any standard that Griselda or her friends would ever consider, rich. Their house had a road to it and gates protecting people from it. They drove around in a Rolls Royce.

They had four children. Roberto and Loretta, the twins and the oldest. Maria, the middle child at twelve years old, and Alejandro, who everyone called Alex, was the youngest at ten years old. Often ignored by his siblings, Alex learned early to play by himself. A quiet boy, with an even quieter demeanor, his family did much to keep him away from the dangers of Colombian life. Things like the constant political violence between the fractured governments of the country. Like the spate of kidnappings that were becoming more and more commonplace. He was a cute boy, brown shaggy hair and oval faced, cherub cheeks his grandmother liked to squeeze. His parents, aware of the dangers, kept him on a tight leash. No going out without his older brother or sister or accompanied by an adult. No talking to strangers. No playing with children that weren't in his neighborhood. No... the list went on and on. And Alex, mostly, followed the rules.

The one time he broke the rule was with Griselda.

When Markos took the group into the upper echelons of Medellin, with an invitation from his old wealthy friends, they'd dress up in their best clothes, mingle, swim in pools, and eat fancy food they'd never eat. Markos would keep Rafi and Jacko from their more asshole-esque qualities in check. It was during one of these parties that they were invited to that Alex met Griselda. They were standing in a large backyard and she had wandered from her friends, dressed in her best dress, where there were more kids her own age. Markos would wink at her when he'd explain to his friends that she and Maggie had to come because otherwise they couldn't come. And his friends would roll their eyes and push Maggie and Griselda to their younger siblings. Griselda didn't care as long as she got the food and got to hang out with Rafi and them. Or, on some occasions, got to jump in a pool and get out of the heat.

Alex, though, for this party, was an actual tag along. His brother reluctantly brought him along, because the rest of the family was busy, and the nanny had a family obligation. His brother didn't want to be bothered with Alex and told him to play with the other kids. But Alex, being shy, was standing off by himself when Griselda walked over to him, smiled at him and said "Hi."

He brightened up immediately and swung around to see her. "Hi," he said a little awkwardly and a little louder than was probably necessary.

"Why are you by yourself?" The other kids were passing a soccer ball back and forth with each other, and Maggie was joining into the game.

"No se," he shrugged.

"You want to kick the ball around?"

"Si," said Alex, grinning wider. "Me llamo Alex."

"Griselda."

11

Alex followed Griselda to the group and they kicked the ball to her and she kicked the ball to Alex and he felt his insides flutter.

After the game, he glued himself to Griselda like a lost puppy. Markos took notice. "Where do you live?"

"Around," she said, forgetting Markos neighborhood.

"I live near El Poblado," Alex said.

"I live around there," she said, if an hour and a half walk was to be considered near. "Not far."

"Really?" Alex asked, excitement filling his eyes.

"Yeah."

"I've never seen you around," he said.

"Do you see everybody that's in El Poblado?"

"No," he said.

"Well, I'm one of those people," said Griselda.

He made a nervous face, like he was worried he had offended her, but she smiled at him, and he felt better. Griselda thought he was kind of goofy in that blind privilege way that kids that didn't live their life could be sometimes. But she still thought he was nice.

He told her where they lived, on Haight St., one of the richer neighborhoods.

"They're rich, rich," said Rafi. "His parents will pay big money for him. We'll all be made. Lydia won't have to whore herself. You'll never have to worry about that. We'll make it like we grabbed you both, so you won't get in trouble. You know what I'm saying? We'll have our faces covered. We'll have a car, a busted-up 40s Renault, but a fucking car. All you have to do is lure him outside and we'll take it from there."

Griselda twisted her foot into the dirt. She didn't want Lydia to end up like her mother, prostituting herself, having to fuck drunk and smelly men for just a few dollars. But she didn't know if she could go along with being a kidnapper, an actual criminal. Stealing food and candy and the occasional article of clothing was one thing. But stealing a whole child? A child her age? That was something else entirely.

"Please Griselda," Lydia begged. "We're going to demand ten thousand American dollars. According to Markos, it will be a drop in the bucket for them. But it will transform our lives. We'll give you a thousand dollars when they pay. We all could get out of here. All of us. Disappear and never be in these fucking slums again."

The idea of a thousand dollars sounded insane to her. A thousand dollars really could change her and her mother's life. She had never even seen that much money in her life or thought about that much money outside of her most vivid dreams. "And no one's going to get hurt?" she asked meekly, trying as she might to convince herself that this was the right thing to do.

"No, honey… we're not monsters," Lydia said.

"I'd never think you guys were monsters," Griselda said.

Lydia grabbed her hands in hers, those soft, but rough fingers gripping her tight, and the slight press of her thumbs into Griselda's palms made her feel good inside. "I know sweety. I know. They'll pay. He'll be back in two days. We're going to keep him in Markos's place. His mother is off caring for her mother and he stayed to make sure no one steals their stuff, so Alejandro will have a bed, food, everything. You'll be with him. It won't be an issue. This will be the easiest thing in the world to change all our lives," said Lydia, squatting down to face Griselda, and stare hopefully in her eyes.

Griselda nodded and smiled. "I'll do it," she said.

4)

Rafi and Lydia donned masks with Markos and Jacko, while Maggie and Yessica were setting up the room to hold Alex in Markos's house. Griselda didn't bother to tell her mother that she was going to be gone for a little while, outside of saying just that. "I'll be with friends for a couple of days." It wasn't like her mother would miss her. And wouldn't be the first time she stayed out with her friends through the night. Her mother wasn't the kind of woman that really worried about her. If she disappeared, Griselda wasn't sure her mother would even look for her.

Griselda couldn't believe the house Alex lived in. They drove by it once, planning their route, noting difficult turns in case they had to flee. The thing was a veritable mansion, huge and expansive, bigger than anything that they had. He was sitting on a tire swing. His nanny was supposed to be watching him but was inside preparing him lunch. He had short hair and a small nose, with a soft maple-hue to his complexion. In another world where they were equal and where Griselda could go to school like he probably did, they could've been friends.

"You remember what you're going to do?" Markos asked.

"Get him out of the yard and to walk with me down the street and then you're going to grab us both."

"Exactly," said Lydia, giving Griselda a kiss on her forehead. "This is going to work out perfectly for all of us, you know. This is the best thing to do. We're going to make money. He'll be home to his family. Okay? No worries."

Griselda nodded her head. She could do this. She would do this. They could escape this life together. She didn't want Lydia to have the fate that ruined her mother and Lydia's mother. More than that. She wanted that money. Wanted to never struggle like she's always struggled. She wanted to be free from the slums, from the poverty, from the hunger, from all of it. The dirt that seemed to never wash off that was poverty.

Getting out of the Renault, she fixed the small summer dress Rafi and Lydia gave her from Maggie's clothes, 'cause she didn't have any other nice clothes. The red dirt that covered the road felt different between her feet, like she was sinking into it. Her stomach felt nervous. What if they got caught? What would happen to her? What would happen to her friends? She couldn't bear to think of that. But there was no turning back. She looked behind her one last time, seeing them in the car, fixing their masks before driving off down the road.

Griselda walked over to the fence, her hands gripping the iron, as she leaned forward, and she quietly called to him, so not to alert his nanny. "Alejandro," she said in a sing-song whisper. "Alex!"

Alex spun himself on his tire to face the fence. The moment he saw Griselda, Alex's entire expression changed from the sullen and bored expression that was consistently plastered across his face to an excited, jovial, wide-eyed happiness. His mouth opened wide and he smiled. "It's you!" he shouted excitedly.

Griselda put her fingers to her lips. "Shh!" she quieted him. She waved her hand rapidly, urging him forward. "Come here! Come here!"

Alex slid himself from the tire and stared at the window of the kitchen where his Nanny hummed happily, and cooked unawares. He jogged over. He was wearing a red jumper and buckled shoes. "Hola," said Griselda.

"You said you lived close, but I still never saw you, and I was looking. But you're here…"

"I, um, you know, um, actually moved just down the street."

"Really?" There was such excitement and hope in this revelation.

"Yeah," Griselda said nervously.

"That's great. We should, you know, play together sometime."

"You want to show me around the neighborhood?"

"My nanny's making lunch. I can ask her if she made enough for you, too."

"I'm enjoying walking and I want to get to know my neighborhood. I could use a boy around to protect me and show me what's what," she said, reaching through the bar and grabbing his hand.

"My Nandy'll be mad."

Griselda squeezed his hand and pulled him closer to her. "It's okay… I'll just look around myself… I'll look for you some other time, if I can find my way back here, though I'm not sure…" She didn't know what else to do, so she started to walk away.

"Wait!" Alex said. She stopped. Griselda looked over her shoulder and smiled. "I'll come."

Her grin grew wider. "Great…"

She followed him around the fence to the gate, where he pressed a button, and the gate started opening. She had never seen anything like it. So much wealth. So many things that she never even thought she'd own in her life. He squeezed through the gate before it opened all the way and he could hear his heart beat like a snare drum in his chest, never having done anything like this before. Adrenaline rush through his body, as he excitedly made his way to her. "So where do you live?"

"I don't know the street," she said. "But I know how to get back to it."

"Okay."

They began walking down the road together, side by side. "You're going to love this neighborhood. There are some great food shops that my mother takes us to."

"Where is your mother?"

"I don't know. She goes out and comes back with lots of bags and my padre always gets angry when she does and tells her that she's going to bankrupt them. Then at night they fight and mom's always screaming to God and daddy's always cursing."

Griselda just laughed. "Mi madre doesn't work," she said. "Mi padre, though, works so much that he's never around most of the time."

"I'm sorry. That's bad." There was a pep in Alex's step as he looked at Griselda, excited by his new friend. She ran ahead of him and he ran after her. "My house is just up here," she said.

With their masks on, the group was ready to go, even though they were sweating up a storm. The material from the masks stuck to their face. They couldn't afford ski-masks and went with old t-shirts. They cut holes at the eyes and mouth, tying it in a knot in the back of their head. "You sure you're a good driver, in case someone calls the cops and we have to get away?"

"I'm a great driver. I drove mi tio home dozens of times when he was too drunk to drive. Don't worry. Just snatch the kid as fast as you can and put this to his head," said Markos, taking a gun out and brandishing it.

"What the fuck are you doing with that?" asked Lydia. "No one's supposed to get hurt."

"Yeah, but we need to make it real, and we need to scare him," said Markos, a sharpness in his voice at being second guessed.

"It's fine! It's fine!" said Rafi, taking the gun and putting it below the window. "It's always good to be prepared for shit and the more the kid's looking at the gun, the less he's looking at us."

Lydia shook her head nervously, not liking how many things were changing, but they were in now, and there was little she could do about it to stop it. They were doing this for her, after all. Well, for all of them, but for her especially. She'd do anything to not have to walk the streets and fuck drunk and ugly men for money.

She saw the car and tried to ignore it as they came up behind them. "Do you have any food at home?" Alex asked.

"Yeah, plenty, a whole –"

Rafi and Lydia jumped from the vehicle. Lydia grabbed the boy and dragged him into the backseat of the car, clasping her hand around his mouth and nose and tying his arms with hers. While Rafi grabbed Griselda and yanked her into his lap in the front seat, his hand wrapped around her mouth, and his other hand around her stomach. She never had been so close to Rafi and she could feel her cheeks blush and her body warm in a weird way as her stomach nervously churned. "Keep your fucking mouth shut, boy, or we'll kill you and the girl," Rafi growled in a much deeper and darker voice that Griselda almost believed.

Markos slammed his foot on the gas. The engine revved, and Griselda fell back into Rafi's chest even harder. He brought his mouth to her ear. "Just stay quiet. Don't say anything," he said and she nodded.

5)

They tossed him into the bedroom and locked the door and kept Griselda outside the room with them. "If one of you tries to escape, the other one dies," said Jacko with a twisted grin, made scarier by the torn hole for his mouth. He grabbed Alex by the face, squeezing his cheeks between his fingers. "Do you understand?" he growled.

Tears poured from the Alex's eyes, as he whimpered and looked to Griselda and nodded his head, before they shoved him backwards into the room, and shut the door. The girls, Maggie and Yessica had hammered wood over the windows, after stuffing blankets inside them, to make it as soundproof as possible. For Alex, not just being abducted, but being placed in such poverty was terrifying for him. The room was dark and it smelled like wet wood. Dust covered the floor. The mattress was thin and wood panels held up the frame, giving it a hard and uncomfortable feeling as he went and sat on it. Why was this happening? He wondered. Why him? Why Griselda? Why? He pressed his hands into his face and wept, wanting something or someone to save him, and worried no one would. He should've listened to his parents, he thought. Never leave the property without someone with you. Now look what happened.

Griselda was worried. She didn't want Alex to get hurt. She didn't think that he deserved to get hurt and she didn't like how rough they were being with him. They got him here. He was their prisoner. They didn't need to be mean about it. And though she knew it was all for show, she didn't like that they kept threatening her. This was a completely different side of her friends. Something violent and desperate. They stayed quiet as they paced, listening for any movement in the room, until finally they were sure that he would not try to escape or scream. Then they walked outside the house, taking off their masks, and breathing fresh air. After nearly forty minutes of breathing through the shirts they wrapped around their heads, even the mildewy and rusting smell of the slums was a welcome change.

Markos pulled a joint from his pocket and lit it, handing it to Rafi first, then it went around the entire group, "Now what?" Rafi asked Markos.

"We make a phone call, tell them no cops, and that we want $10,000 American Dollars for their son back. I'll drive by the house to make sure they don't have any of the police, and we'll go from there."

"What if they do have the cops?"

"Who's going to risk their child's life like that?"

"Our mother," said Rafi and Lydia.

"Mine too," said Yessica.

"With them…"

"That's cause we're poor," said Markos. "They have money, they'll pay the money, all they want is their kid back. It'll be fine."

"Do you have their phone number?"

Markos paused.

"We don't have their fucking number?!"

"No… okay, I forgot about finding out their number. But… the kid should know."

"We're getting off to a great start."

"Can we not be so rough?" Griselda asked. "I think he'll help, you know, without being mean to him."

"Being mean to him," Jacko said, "will keep him in line. Don't be a baby, Griselda."

"I'm not a baby."

"Well, don't whine about something stupid," said Jacko.

"I wasn't whining."

"Cool it, man. We wouldn't even have him if it wasn't for Griselda," said Rafi, wrapping an arm around her shoulder and putting the joint in her mouth. She sucked on the joint and felt like she was giving his fingers a kiss in the process and liked it. He spun Griselda around and squatted down in front of her. "You did great. We're not going to hurt him. I promise. But Jacko's right, we don't want him thinking that we're not going to hurt him. Because then he'll just become stubborn. We need him to be obedient. We need you to just keep playing your role, okay?"

"Yeah," Lydia said. "We're not going to hurt him. But they're both right. The more scared he is, the more likely he is to follow our orders without problems or

21

hassles. Don't worry. We've got this. We're almost there. We just got to get his family's phone number."

6)

"What do you mean you don't know your fucking phone number?" shouted Jacko in Alex's face, his hand tightening up into a fist.

Alex curled himself into a frightened, whining, simpering ball and squealed anxiously. "I don't know. I don't know. They changed it. I never use a phone."

"You better fucking remember, or you're worthless to us, and that means…" Jacko drew the blade of his hand across his throat and Alex whined even more.

Jacko came through the door with Markos and slammed it shut frustratedly. "Fuck!" he screamed. "This fucking sucks."

"What the hell are we supposed to do now?" said Lydia.

"I don't know. I don't know. We'll send them a letter or something. You know. Go drop a letter off at his house."

"What if there are cops there?"

"Then we drop it in the mail or something, tell them to get rid of the cops, and to pay us the fucking money," said Markos frustratedly. His hands ran through his black hair nervously, his stomach knotting. It was all falling apart. It was all coming undone. Griselda felt sick. She knew they shouldn't have done this, that they weren't kidnappers. That they were just kids in a shitty situation. They were going to be put in prison, executed, something. They didn't know what was going to happen, but they figured it wouldn't be good.

Lydia paced outside, wanting to scream, but not wanting to draw anymore attention to themselves than they were doing already. Not that many people took time to notice anything that was going around in their slum. As both a professional courtesy and for their own safety. "We're fucked. I'm fucked. You fucked us estupido. You didn't get their fucking number. Their number!"

"I thought he would know it," groaned Markos.

"Well, we got to do something," said Rafi. "We got to get a letter together, or something."

"I got an idea," said Yessica. "What if we give Griselda the note? She's already got the nice clothes and everything. She has that innocent look. Her home is away enough from here so if the police follow her back, she can take them back to her house. And we give her like a few dollars and she says some guy approached her and offered her money to drop off the letter. Just a big man, goatee, brown skin, with a scar over his right eye through his eyebrow. Something like that. Easy. They can't hold her. They aren't going to question anything. They'll take her home."

Griselda listened, but didn't like the idea. This wasn't the plan at all. She was supposed to be done. There wasn't supposed to be any more for her part. She did her part. "Why can't Maggie do it?"

"Cause Maggie lives shacks down from here. You live on the other side. The odds that they'll connect us are zilch, but Maggie has a direct connection. Where's your brother? Where's your sister? You don't have that."

"What if they don't believe me? What if they arrest me?" Griselda started whimpering and shaking her head, turning her back, not wanting to look like a baby in front of her friends. She hated crying. Her mother always reprimanded her for it, spanked her, slapped her, beat her.

"Don't cry," said Lydia. "Remember what the goal is. Ten thousand American dollars. Look, you're doing more work. We'll give you two thousand dollars. Two thousand dollars when we get paid. You can get out of here. We all can, and all of us can have a better life."

She wiped her nose across her arm and rubbed it against the dress. "I don't want to go to jail."

"Well, if we don't get some way to contact them and keep them from involving the police, we're going to go to jail, regardless."

"But –"

Rafi came over to where she was sitting and leaned himself in front of her. "Look… know this isn't what we planned, but it's still going to work, and you're still going to be safe. Okay? You are. It's fine. I promise it. We need you to do this. Lydia needs you to do this. I need you to do this… okay, kiddo? Please?"

She couldn't stare into his eyes and say no. His crooked teeth made for a pleasant smile, nonetheless. Those hazel brown eyes just held her like he was trying to hypnotize her, and it was working. "Okay. Okay… I'll do it."

They stood up, excited like the first time. Rafi gave her a kiss on her cheek and her face turned rosy red. *Two thousand dollars*, she reminded herself. *Two thousand American dollars*. Her mom and she could move back to Cartagena, or go somewhere else entirely. Two thousand dollars could probably get them to America itself. Whatever it could do, it could get them away from where they were. And in the end, that's all that mattered to her. That's all that could matter.

7)

Markos dropped her off a half mile from the house and she walked the rest of the way, clenching the letter they composed tight to her chest. By the time she got to the house, there were police already in the driveway. Their cars standing as a threat to everything that Griselda was trying to do. Lying, though, lying was something that had always come naturally to her. Lying, for better or worse, seemed to be her super power. Where other people had feelings of guilt or shame, she experienced excitement when she knew she was getting over on someone. And though she was scared... terrified, really... Griselda kept walking forward.

Because of the police being there, the gate was open. Griselda's stomach was a tangled mess of stress and worry. Unsure what was going to happen as she walked up the cobblestone driveway, past the well-pruned hedges, and over to the gorgeous wooden steps of the house. She was keenly aware of an officer staring at her as he stood at the patrol car, unsure who she was. Unperturbed, she proceeded up to the door, and she knocked on the door and the door opened. A tearful, worried woman, wearing a similar bob as Griselda answered, as she wiped at her mascara-stained face. "I got told to give you this letter," she said and held out the piece of paper.

She grabbed the letter and read it. Griselda stood there, playing innocent, her eyes cast down. The woman, in a moment, paused as she finished the letter, and an instant later, her face melted in panic and she seized Griselda by the arms. "Who told you to give me this letter? Where's Alejandro? Where's my son?"

Officers rushed over and grabbed the girl away from Alex's mother and, once they had calmed her down, they turned their attention to Griselda. They brought her into the house. There was a coolness to it. Fans rotated overhead in wishing and whirring, frosty glasses with ice cubes sat on the table. Lightbulbs decorated the interior, cutting through the darkness that was building outside. The officers brought her into the kitchen, telling her, "It's okay, honey. You're not in trouble. We just want to know what happened to the boy."

"I don't know about any boy," she said. Her friends had told her, no matter what, no matter what they say, always repeat that you have no idea who 'THE BOY' is. Don't try to be familiar. The officers patted her back, treated her with kid gloves they never treated her with when they saw her on the street.

They fetched her a glass of juice. She only got juice on special occasions in the shanties.

An officer stood in front of her. He was a tall man, with a large round nose, and a darker than usual face. "I'm officer Rodrigo. What's your name?"

"Griselda?" she said in an uncertain tone. She rubbed her hands together and as Lydia told her to do, she started sniffling and pretending to cry. "I..." Sniffle. "Didn't mean to do anything bad..." Sniffle, sniffle. "I didn't do anything. I just was told to deliver the letter." She put her face in her hands and started sobbing. Scared. Nervous. And yet, at the same time, the idea that she was going to lie to them, that she was going to get away, excited her. She knew she could do it.

"Don't cry honey. You're not in trouble. Griselda... you said?" She looked up at officer Rodrigo and nodded. "That's a pretty name."

She smiled at the police officer. "Gracias."

"Where do you live, Griselda?"

"Near Comuna 13," she said.

"You're pretty far from there."

"A man took me in his car, a red car... mi papi had one... it starts with an R... something..."

"A Renault?"

"Si, si," she said, looking up, partially smiling, and partially sad. "He asked me to deliver a letter for him."

"A man?"

"Si."

"What type of man?"

"Que?"

"What did he look like?"

"He had a beard on the front of his face. He was older. Like your age older. He was big but not like fat big but like big and tall. Smelly. He was very smelly."

"Smelly?"

"Si... like um, fish, stinky fish. He smelled like stinky fish. I hate fish. It's so stinky and that's what he smelled like."

"Did you know him?"

Griselda shook her head rapidly.

"Then why get in his car? Did he grab you?"

She shook her head again.

"Then what happened?"

Griselda reached into the pocket of her dress and held out her other hand and showed the crinkled pesos.

"He gave me money and said that if I deliver the letter I could keep it. I don't have lots of money."

"A man gave you money?"

"Yeah. He came up to me in a red car and he asked me if I wanted to make some money to help my family. He said he needed to drop off a letter to some people, but didn't want them to know it was him that dropped it off. He said it would be a big favor and make lots of people happy. I just wanted to make people happy."

"And you never saw him around Comune 13 before."

"I don't know."

"You don't know?"

"I don't think so."

"You don't think so?"

"No... I don't... I don't know. I uh, I never saw him before. Am I in trouble? I just wanted to have money to see a movie. To give to mi madre. To help." She sniffled and forced her eyes to water even more. "I'm sorry. I didn't know I was doing bad. I didn't know!" she screamed.

"No, no," the officer said, stepping back from Griselda as she wept and screamed, burying her face in her hands, and trying her best to look completely inconsolable. "It's okay, Griselda. It's okay. How 'bout we take you home and drive you around the area and you see if you can spot the car or the man? Would you do that for us?"

Griselda wondered if she played the part a little too well. Nervousness ripped into her. But she nodded. "Good... good... let's do that then."

8)

For over two hours they drove her around Comune 13, twice passing by Markos's shanty where she knew Alex was, but she proudly didn't even look in that direction. There was a twisted thrill, being the kidnapper, and being along with the police to catch herself. This is something her young mind didn't quite process and she wouldn't understand until she was much older and her relationship with the police was even more hostile.

Driving through the town in the dark drew the ire of the criminal element, who would spit at the car as it drove by. Officer Rodrigo felt bad for Griselda. Growing up in a place like this. Figuring correctly that she didn't have any schooling or education, probably couldn't read or write, which built credence to her story in his mind. "Who do you live with?" Rodrigo asked her, rubbing her arm and offering an awkward smile.

"Mi madre."

"And what does your madre do?"

"She has friends over that leave her money when they leave. I go in a closet when they're over."

Rodrigo nodded. He didn't say anything. He didn't know what there was to say. He should be used to it. To the stories. To the stuff he hears and witnesses, but the cherub face little child seemed so lost and innocent, it reminded him of his own daughter.

She kept having them slow down and through tinted glass, she would look at someone, and then saying that it wasn't him because he lacked a scar, or a beard, or wasn't heavy enough, but she kept picking men that looked vaguely like the description she made, until eventually Officer Rodrigo took her home. He walked her up the narrow steps, over to her small dilapidated home, and to the door. He knocked and her mother answered.

Ana Blanco was beautiful once. In her youth, her face was taut, her breasts perky, and there was a flare for life that danced in her eyes. But years of alcohol had weighed heavily on her appearance. Her stomach bulged slightly, a cigarette danced between her chapped lips, nail polish was chipped away at, and her breasts sagged in the halter top she donned. "Que? What are you doing with my daughter?"

"A man picked your daughter up to deliver a letter about a kidnapped boy. We hoped she could help us."

"You think my daughter a snitch? What you going to do if these men know she's working with the police and come here and murder us? You drive her through the neighborhood, walk her to the door, in a fucking police car. Are you mad?"

"There's a missing boy."

"Children go missing here all the time," Ana said drunkenly, taking a swig from a bottle that was gripped tightly in her left hand as she pulled the cigarette out with the other. "Where are the policia then? Que? Donde?"

Rodrigo grimaced. He knew this was going to go nowhere. "Do you own a car?" he asked.

"Que? Does it look like I can afford a car? Eres estupido. Get away from my daughter." She grabbed Griselda by the arm and yanked her into the house and slammed the door into Rodrigo's face. The last he heard was Ana's yelling. "You bring the cops to our home. Our home. You want us to starve? To get murdered!"

"I'm sorry, momma!" Griselda screamed as her mother brought one slap after another down across her body and face. Her mother never held back when she got into a mood. Griselda knew that. It was the one thing, though, that Griselda didn't fully think on. So tied up in thinking about getting over on the police, she forgot that her mother would be furious she was anywhere near police.

"If people think police are coming here. They won't come here. And if they don't come here, we don't have money to eat, you stupid puta!" Ana screamed, tossing Griselda onto a makeshift couch in the corner, and continuing to swing her open hand at her.

"Mommy, Mommy!" Griselda screamed. "Please mommy! Please! I just wanted to get you money. Money, see, money!" She held up the crinkled pesos that Officer Rodrigo gave her as they took the others for evidence.

Her mother stopped for a moment, snatching the money from her hand and counting it. "This will not feed us for an entire day. You risk my work for this?" She tossed the money back at Griselda's face. "Where did you get this dress?"

"A friend."

"Friend?"

"Si, mi amigos. Please madre. Please… I'm sorry!" Griselda screamed. "I'm sorry! I'll never do it again. I promise. I promise!"

Ana stared at her daughter, crying and sniveling, her cheeks and arms red from her lashing, and a wave of annoyance washed over her. "Go, get in the closet, and stay there for the rest of the night. I got to go and get work and pray no one really took notice since it's so early. Not a peep. Not a sound. You hear me, Griselda? You hear me?!"

"Si Madre!" Griselda said, trying to stop herself from crying more, knowing her mother hated when she cried.

With that, her mother put down the bottle of alcohol and stubbed the cigarette out in an ashtray. She had a mirror set up next to a candle and looked at herself. Fixing her hair, dabbing on her make-up, all the while Griselda watched silently. It was like Griselda didn't even exist anymore. Like she wasn't even a thought.

Ana used her fingers to wipe away some lipstick that wavered too far from her lips and then slinked her way to the door and grabbed a pair of heels. "You go to the closet. If I see you before the morning, I'll assume you want to join me in working."

Griselda swallowed back a tearful nausea and jumped from the couch and moved hastily to the closet. As she shut the door on herself and encased herself in darkness, she thought about Alejandro, about his mother's response, about how much she cared and missed him, and a piece of her hated Alex for that. He had money and love. Two things she'd never experienced. Sitting with her thoughts, she was sure he deserved this... His whole family deserved this.

9)

For the next two days, Griselda stayed away from her friends and wondered if the letter work. They were supposed to paint their number on the outside of the house, on their fence, in big bright numbers, for someone to call them. She didn't know if they did it. She didn't know what was happening. She went through her day for the next two days like nothing had changed in her life. Sat in the closet at night, listening to her mother's work. And on the third day, when she was certain that the cop wasn't coming back or watching her anymore, she made her way carefully over to her friend's place, taking routes through grimy back passageways they would often run through if they were chased by a store keep. Even if Officer Rodrigo was watching her, he wouldn't be able to keep up with her, as she maneuvered her way through one dank alleyway after another, until she made it back to Markos's little home.

They were all there, smoking weed, jittery and nervous. "Did they, um... you know... do it?" Griselda asked as she closed the door behind her.

None of them looked like they were sitting on ten thousand dollars and happy, so she didn't think the answer to this question was going to be yes, but she wanted to be optimistic. "Everything's fucked," said Lydia.

"Porque?"

"They don't want to pay. They're refusing to pay. And they traced the car back to Markos's uncle when we drove by and got the number. Markos's uncle beat the shit out of him pretty badly for stealing his car and making him have to deal with the police."

"So, what are we going to do? Are we just going to let him go?"

"That's the problem," said Rafi. "He tried to escape, and he saw our faces. Saw that you're not here with us. He knows you. And now the police know you from dropping the letter off and everything."

"What are you saying?" she asked.

Jacko took his gun, a small revolver, and put it on the table. "We need to kill him."

"No!" said Griselda. "That's not what we're supposed to do!"

"They're not paying. We can't be in the slums, hiding from the police, when they know we're in the slums hiding from them. They'll find us. They'll find us and they'll put us in fucking prison, or they'll execute us. We've got to make him disappear, so he never speaks again. That's the only way. The only way," said Lydia.

"So, who's going to do it?"

"If any of us do it and it's discovered, we'll be put to death," said Rafi. "But if you did it, if you went in there and pulled the trigger, there's nothing the law would do to you. And we'll make sure the body is never found. We'll bury it in the dumps, in the ground, in the middle of the night."

"Why not Maggie?" Griselda asked. "Why me?"

"We asked Maggie to do it, but she couldn't. She tried. She really tried. But she couldn't. She's not strong like you," said Lydia. Griselda liked the compliment. "She's not there yet. You're like us. You've been through shit just like us. You could do it. You could do it and we could all be safe."

"But..."

"It's fine," said Rafi. "You don't have to either. We shouldn't have asked. We got into this mess. If we get caught, I guess we deserve the death penalty." His voice was low and saccharine. "It's not your responsibility, it's ours. We shouldn't have asked you that. We just… everything is just so out of hand."

"I don't know how to use a gun," Griselda said.

"It's okay. I mean, it's easy to use." Rafi picked the gun up and walked over to her. He walked behind her and he reached his arms around her body and put the gun in her hands and pointed it away from everyone. He took her hands in his and placed it on the gun, taking her finger and putting it lightly on the trigger. "Don't squeeze it. Just keep your finger there. It's okay." Slowly, he lifted his hands from hers, leaving her pointing the gun at the door. It was heavier than it looked. Colder too. For some reason, she always thought a gun would feel hot in the hands. But she wouldn't be surprised if it was the coolest thing in the shanty. "You pull back the hammer. Aim it. And pull the trigger. And it's done, just like that. Over. We'll take care of the rest."

She looked down the small snub-nose barrel at the small sight at the tip. The idea of losing her friends, especially when they were the only ones she had, was more frightening to Griselda than the act itself. Spending the last two days in the closet, knowing how he lived, knowing that his parents didn't care enough to hand over the money. Maybe he was better off dead, she thought to herself. He wasn't like them. He was too soft for this world. Too soft for this life. And in Medellin, in Colombia, being soft was a death sentence. If it wasn't her, she figured, it'd be someone else, eventually. There would always be someone else.

Griselda walked over to the door, the gun to her side, and she opened the door. She found Alejandro, his face bruised, his eye swollen, hiding in the corner.

"Alex…" she called to him, putting the gun behind her. "Alex, it's me, Griselda."

"Griselda," he mumbled into his arms, lifting his face cautiously, and looking at her. "You're okay. Are they letting us go?" His whimper made her not like him even more. He had money, luxury… he had fans to keep himself cool in the endless Colombian heat, and all it's done for him, is make him a sniveling coward, she thought. He didn't deserve the comfort. He didn't deserve the wealth. And his family didn't deserve him.

"Yeah," she said. "My parents paid."

"They did? For both of us?"

He got to his feet. A bloody nose made the bottom half of his face look cherry in the darkness of the room and the blood covered the front of his shirt, now dried and dark and brown. He stood in front of her. Relief, a lot of relief on his face. "Yea, you're going to be fine. We're both going to be fine." He froze as he stood in front of her and she brought the gun to her side.

"What's that?"

She stared into Alex's eyes and raised the gun.

His eyes went wide, but before his mouth could open to speak, before the shock wore off, the gun exploded in a loud, deafening eruption, that went through Griselda's entire body, sending pain shooting through her shoulders, as the gun jerked up, and the bullet shot right into Alex's face. The boy crumpled backwards to the floor, blood beginning to pour from his head, and she stood there, unsure what she just did. Unsure how to respond. Unsure if she could ever be normal again.

Rafi came in first, with Lydia behind him, and he took the gun from Griselda. "I can't believe you did it," he said.

"You told me to."

"No, no, it's not bad," Rafi said. "You're just something special, Griselda. Something special!"

Lydia froze when she walked into the room. She stared at the boy's lifeless body. At the way his eyes were already beginning to pale in his death, his skin becoming pallid, and she fought back the sickness that roiled up in her stomach like a churning sea. She turned and left the room and left the house.

"I did what you wanted," Griselda said meekly, as Rafi took the gun from her.

"I know you did. We all know you did."

"Did I do bad?"

"No," said Rafi.

"You shot him right between the eyes," Jacko said with some amusement.

Yessica pushed through and her face paled when she saw the boy, but unlike Lydia, she didn't flee. Instead, what fright she had soon turned to fascination, as Rafi led Griselda out of the room, putting the gun in his pocket.

"You go home, Griselda. Don't say anything to anyone. Don't tell anyone anything. Stay low, quiet, and don't say a word. We'll take care of the rest. Okay?"

Griselda nodded. Her body tingled. Her hands wouldn't stop shaking. She killed him. She actually killed him. Alejandro Ribaldi was dead because of her. And though she often thought that such things should make her feel guilty or bad, or at least like Lydia, puking on the corner of the shanti, trying to keep it from going in her hair, she felt none of those things. Not one bit. There was a coldness to it she didn't expect. It was done and over with and she was here and he was not. Lydia glanced up at Griselda, then looked away again.

"I'm sorry we couldn't get you money," Rafi said.

"Me too," said Griselda.

Maybe that was the worst of it. Maybe that's what made her feel so bad. She didn't even get the money. Nothing. All of that for nothing. He was dead for nothing. It was all an enormous waste of time. And it sucked.

Griselda walked home and went into her own shanty where her mother lay sleeping, waiting for the night to come, a bottle beside her, and bottles covering the floor. Griselda climbed on the couch and she laid there, replaying the killing again and again. If she kills someone again, she was going to make sure to get something out of it. That was sure, she told herself. That was damn sure.

PART 2
A GIRL'S FIRST LOVE
RAFI

CHAPTER 2

1) 1956

Griselda knew the day would come like it did for a lot of young girls in their shanty community that was her home. The day she'd be used to help bring in more money for the family. When her mother would no longer allow her to "Live off her," if what you could call her life living. She'd remember it forever. The first man. Only thirteen years old, just beginning to blossom into a woman, her breasts only beginning to show beneath her shirts.

The man was American. He wore a suit. He was skinny and pale. The tip of his nose and his cheeks were sunburned and had a reddish hue to them. He smelled like whiskey.

Her mother put her make-up on, blush on her cheeks, rosy gloss on her lips. She fit her into one of her outfits that hung off her, as she hadn't yet fully grown into the body her mother had, even though they were nearly the same height. Ana combed Griselda's hair, kissed her on the top of her head, and it was the kindest that her mother had ever been with her.

The man was nervous, maybe even more so than Griselda. Rubbing his hands together and taking quick glances at the child that he was about to enjoy... wondering, maybe, if he should go through with this or not.

41

Griselda had watched what happened between her mother and these men many times through the crack in the closet. She had listened to Lydia tell about the men she was with each night... Poor Lydia. She had become so jaded and angry, smoking cigarettes in the afternoon, as she waited for the night to come. She had tons of stories. Some timid and some gross. From men who climbed on and off in the span it took her to get comfortable, to men who enjoyed being spit on, or having their manhood sucked upon.

Griselda had heard lots of stories, seen lots of things, and was very sure she knew what to expect.

A burning sensation, especially for the first time, a bit of sharp pain. That's what Lydia said. "Most guys are quick," she said. "Especially if you moan. And especially if they're foreigners. If you moan, they'll tip you a lot of time. Just don't cry. Most men hate that. The ones that like it... those guys are scary a lot of time."

"I'm Peter," said the man, reaching his hand out to Griselda. Her mother glared at her, and she slowly took his hand in hers.

"Hola señor," she said. "Me llamo Griselda."

"Hola Griselda," he said and grinned, nodding to Ana that he was ready to be left alone.

Ana nodded and walked from the shanty. Griselda stared at the man, as his fingers played with the thin soft material of the nightgown that her mother put on her. Her mother had contemplated shaving her between her legs, but the small fuzz that was beginning to grow there made her think it would sell the innocence far more. Especially since the man didn't want a child, just something young. That it was her first time, made for a bigger payday. Fifty American dollars.

Griselda would remember later that his hands were clammy. That he sweat a lot. That he tasted salty when she kissed him, and saltier still when she took him into her mouth, like her mother had told her to do. She liked it when he went between her legs. The feeling was unique. Initially, she shivered and wiggled, and a chill ran down her spine. But the more he stayed down there, the better she began to feel.

The pain when he was on top of her was minimal. Like Lydia said it would be. And as she heard her mother do so many times, she moaned along with him, keeping her legs parted, while he slobbered messily on her chest. When it was over and he was getting dressed, he reached into his pocket and pulled out a ten-dollar bill and tossed it at her. "That was fun," he said. "You were very nice, Griselda. It was a pleasure meeting you."

She laid on the bed for a while. Her sex throbbing. A little blood seeping from her violated body. She stared at the ceiling and thought back to when she was eleven and how all of this could've been different if they had just paid. She didn't think about that often. Rarely at all. More times than not, she even questioned whether it even happened. But for right now, while the man left, and Ana walked him out, Griselda laid naked and bare to the world, wondering if she had gotten that two thousand dollars, if this would've ever happened.

"I knew you weren't a waste of flesh and bone," she said, fanning the fifty dollars in cash that he gave her. This would cover food and the cost of the shanty for months. "You did good." She grabbed the ten dollars off the bed as Griselda felt hot tears slip down her face and pool in her ears. She held back crying for as long as she could. She waited until he was gone.

"Get up. I need to clean the bedding. You bled too goddamn much. Go clean yourself out. I got a douche in the sink. You'll be fine and you'll get used to it," Ana said bitterly.

Griselda rolled gingerly onto her side, then on to her feet. She kept her legs spread and walked gingerly forward. She shut the door while her mother stripped the bed.

2) 1957

Griselda woke up with a hand being pressed to her mouth and her underwear being pushed aside. It was early in the morning; the sun was just up, but cast against the back of the Shanty, and only a few hints of light through the openings outside. She clenched her jaw as the man worked his way between her thighs and shoved his underwear down his legs. This had been happening weekly now. If it wasn't enough that she had to take Johns when her mother was coming up short on money, her mother's boyfriend couldn't keep his hands off of her either.

She wondered why she stayed. She really did. But, fashioning herself as a realist, even at the young age of fourteen, Griselda knew what the streets had for her. Abduction and violation was common. There was an all-out war happening in civilized society over the liberals and the conservatives. No, the world was just as dangerous and ruthless. Especially for a poor young woman like herself.

The weird thing was that Griselda liked sex. After she had gotten over her new role in life, after it stopped being painful, and she learned to relax into it, it actually became pleasurable sometimes. And with the right guy, with the couple of boys in the neighborhood she chose for herself, she liked it a lot.

Just not always with who she had to do it with, and especially not with Viktor, her mother's boyfriend, who, every time her mother passed out early in the morning, continued to worm his way on the couch that she slept on, and fuck her without a word. The first time he did it, she fought back, until he put his hand tight over her mouth, and another around her throat, gripping it, and threatening to choke her to death if she resisted.

The next half-dozen times she just laid there, waiting for him to finish, imagining ways she would kill him one day. One day, when she knew how to get rid of the body. She imagined maybe she would get revenge on all the people that wronged het. Kill all the men that were disappointments in her life. Kill her mother, even. She thought about that a lot.

But that was all in the future. Far and away from where she was right now. Now, all she had were the small moments of entertainment. Moments with Rafi that she enjoyed the most.

It was Rafi that she liked to have sex with. He was eighteen now. He was a man in every way. He started selling pot and basuco on the streets and was making money. Lots of money. And while Lydia had run off with a John and disappeared in Bogota, taking Maggie with her, he stayed to care for their mother, who got tuberculosis. He felt a loyalty to his mother that Griselda could never muster for her own mother.

Rafi was different from the boy he was three years prior and yet very much the same. He had his rough edges, like most men in his position, and most men that Griselda knew, but he was tender with her. Sweet. He

45

gave her basuco for the first time and she discovered a new love that made everything else easy in life. Drug manufacturers considered Basuco the trash left over during cocaine purification. It was a paste like substance, grayish white, with specks of black, that was usually free based. It was cheaper than coke and more potent, and it made the entire world feel better. It could make sex with the most unattractive and unskilled man amazing.

The first time she had it was the first time she and Rafi had sex. She had come over after a few weeks of not seeing him. Her night job and his kept them sleepy and unproductive in the morning hours. But she woke up early and was bored and didn't want to be alone. Her mother was still passed out on the bed, not that her mother cared where she wandered off to, as long as she brought home money in the morning.

When she knocked on the door, Rafi answered slowly, a gun in his hand. He had grown so much from the fourteen-year-old boy that she fell for at eleven. Tattoos decorated his biceps and chest. He had muscles, visible abs, and he got taller, towering over her five-foot frame. He smiled at her. He was missing two teeth on the right side of his mouth, but it didn't take away from his attractiveness to Griselda.

"Damn girl," Rafi said. "You're looking sexy. You looking to chill or something?"

"Yea, or something," she said.

"You caught me when I just woke up," he said. "Which is good on you, cause I sleep like a fucking log. I swear, cops could kick down my door and they'd think I'm dead or some shit."

She laughed as he walked her over to the couch. It was nice. It was new. Not some makeshift shit like most people, including her, were laying on. The place was decorated. There was a carpet on the floor. Drug dealing was proving very good for him. "You ever try basuco?" he asked

She'd heard of it. Any poor Colombian had heard of it. Seen the addicts laying on the street, with shaky hands, and nervous twitches. But she had never tried it. Never thought about it. Not much. Pot and alcohol were her general drugs of choice. Though she worried about ending up like her mother. A once beautiful woman, slowly destroying herself and becoming less and less attractive.

Rafi ignored her apprehensive words and went over to a dresser in the room and without trying to hide it from her, opened the dresser and pulled the entire drawer out and reached inside and pulled out a plastic bag full of it. He tossed it on the table in front of her. "This shit sells like nothing I've had before. The fucking addicts here eat it up. And the high is fucking amazing. Like one of the best highs I've ever had."

He took a pipe out of his pant pocket and dropped himself beside her. "Do you want to try some with me?" She didn't know why it always felt easy to make dumb choices with him. But it was a constant in her life. She watched Rafi as he looked around and grabbed a small, flat piece of metal. Something she'd seen addicts using in alleyways. He grabbed a lighter on the floor, put some basuco on the piece of metal, hanging the piece of metal partially off the table and started heating it with the lighter. "When it smokes, you want to inhale it through this." He handed Griselda the pipe.

She stared at the grayish goop that began to bubble and melt on the steel. She bent forward and began inhaling the smoke through the pipe. It burnt the back of her throat, more than weed ever did. And it smelled like shit. Her first thought, from the taste, the feeling, the discomfort, was that this wasn't for her. Not at all.

She pushed the smoke out in a cloud, coughing into her hand as she handed the pipe to Rafi. Rafi added more to the metal and kept heating it, and leaned forward. The feeling hit her like a truck. It started as a tingle in her fingertips. Her heart started to speed up. Everything got clearer and her mind snapped awake. She pressed the palms of her hands into her eyes and tossed her head back. Griselda inhaled deeply through her nose and let out a near orgasmic breath. Rafi dropped back beside her.

Rafi's head dropped over to her. "You feeling it, huh?"

"Ay Dios Mios! I feel so good."

Rafi flipped a few strands of Griselda's hair back. "You've grown over the years," he said.

Griselda smiled. "In a lot of ways." She grabbed his hand and brought it to her chest.

"How old are you?"

"Old enough to be on the streets."

"We should've made that money. We would've all been better off."

"Maybe…" said Griselda.

Rafi shifted on the couch, turning and kissing her lips. She liked his mouth. His lips. The look in his eyes. Rafi rolled over more, pulling at her shirt, reaching under it, grabbing her breasts and squeezing them in his hands. She moaned into his mouth. Before she knew it, her leg draped over the frame of the couch, the wood biting into her leg, as Rafi fucked her, grinding on top of her. She'd been with many men at this point.

But none that had felt quite as good as being with Rafi. Maybe it was the basuca, maybe it was the years and years of silently crushing on him, and yearning for him, and wanting him. Maybe it was just the disappointing men that spent their measly money to get between her thighs because they didn't know what to do with women they didn't have to pay. Whatever it was. Whatever the reason. She was hooked to Rafi and found a new high.

3) 1958

The moon was high in the sky, covering the streets in its silvery embrace, while music played from some clubs, pouring out into the streets, while drunk and high individuals sought what pleasure could be had from what was available.

Griselda was looking for work like she always did. Three years now on the street, she was an old pro at it now. She didn't even think about it anymore. She just went with it. One John after another. Taking what time she could to feel normal with her love, with her one and only, Rafi. So, when she saw him leaving a club, dragging on a cigarette, her heart lit-up, as it always did when she saw him. She smiled in his direction and started over to him; her hand up and the words at the back of her throat were about to call out to him. When suddenly she paused. A woman, some puta. Came out of the club, draping a drunkenly sloven arm over his shoulder. She kissed him on the cheek and rubbed her hands down his body. Rage filled Griselda. As the woman moved in front of him and kissed his lips and brought her small narrow mouth to his ear, whispering some enticing words. Griselda's jaw clenched. Her hands balled into fists. She hurried herself across the street, stopping and grabbing a loose brick on the curb. Rafi saw her first and stepped away from the girl on his arm. "Griselda," he tried to coo.

She walked up to the two of them, cursing at him, "You son of a bitch. You ass. You going to play with this puta?"

The woman's hair was dyed blond. She had a hooked nose and was dressed like she was there to get one thing... Rafi. And Griselda wasn't going to allow that.

Rafi was Griselda's. No other bitch was going to have him. The woman turned, furious at being called a puta, and snarled at Griselda. "Tu eres la puta! If anyone would even pay for a bitchy midget coño."

The girl, whoever she was, Griselda didn't bother to get a name, didn't notice the brick in Griselda's hand, at least before Griselda took it across her face.

Blood splattered and the girl screamed as she fell to the ground. The girl buried her face in her hands as blood seeped between her fingers. "You stay the fuck away from my man, or next time, I do more than break your fucking face, you ugly fucking perra." Griselda delivered a sharp kick into the woman's ribs, nearly punting her over onto her back. She drove her foot again and again until Rafi grabbed her. His arms wrapping beneath her breasts and pulled her away from the scene, before more people started to take notice. Before the cops showed up – if they ever showed up in these neighborhoods.

"Get your hands off me," she yelled, struggling against his grip as he dragged her into an alley.

He pressed her against the wall, pushing his hips out as she tried to hit him in the groin. Rafi slapped her. Slapped her hard, grabbing her by the throat. "Stop it!"

he said strictly. "Tu eres loco perra." He slammed his mouth into hers, pressing her lips into her teeth until she tasted blood. She moved her mouth from his and slapped him across the face.

"You want bitches like that?"

Rafi laughed and spun Griselda around. "I want you!" he said. He pressed Griselda's face against the cold brick and hiked her mini-skirt up, reaching beneath the material and grabbing her panties and pulling them down her thighs.

He unzipped his pants and pushed inside of her. His excitement rampant.

Rafi knew what a dangerous game he was playing with Griselda and he enjoyed playing it. For the last two years, whenever they could make time for each other, they would smoke basuco together and then fuck like rabbits and she would orgasm and it would be the only person she would orgasm with. Her toes curled. Her nails dug into his back. And she was in love with him. He loved that she was in love with him.

Rafi loved many things about her, even if he didn't fully love her. Her jealousy and violence were one of the bigger attractions. It made him feel loved. It made her different from any other woman he had met. There was something unique and brutal about her. Something special to her loyalty to him. Something he'd known ever since she killed Alejandro at his request.

Lying next to each other back at his place, smoking more basuco and prepping for a round two, Griselda said, "I could help you sell this stuff; you know."

"Drug dealing is not for girls," said Rafi.

"Fuck you," she said, letting out the smoke. "I could fucking sell more than you could."

"I bet you could."

"How much do you make?"

"Enough."

"What's enough?"

"Enough… Geez… You thinking of robbing me or something?"

"Definitely doing something to you," she laughed, running his hand down his lap. "I just want out of this fucking life."

"I get you. I get you. What do you want me to do?"

"I just need some place to stay. I can figure out my own way to take care of money. I just need to get away from my fucking psycho mother. You know you want this pussy available to you twenty-four-seven… all fucking yours…"

Rafi pulled a joint from his pocket and lit it. He sucked on it and the paper retreated quick and far. Then he exhaled a cloud of smoke. "You're fucking crazy."

"But in the best ways."

"You so fucking jealous." He handed her the joint.

"You like that." She hit the joint.

"I do like that…"

"So…"

"So what?"

4)

Ana Blanco was furious. Her daughter wasn't working. She didn't show back up at the house for two days and then waltzed in as if nothing was wrong, smelling of weed and that distinct smell of smoked cocaine that seemed to sink into the streets. She was pacing in the house. Her boyfriend was back at his shack for the day. It was just the two of them.

Thunder erupted outside. Bottles covered the floor. "Where have you been?" Ana slurred. She leaned herself against the door frame. Her eyes narrowed with a wicked glare that would've cowed most people. But Griselda was far and done with being fearful of her mother.

"Out," said Griselda.

"Out?"

"I was out with a friend."

"How much did you make?"

"I wasn't working."

"What do you mean, you weren't working?"

"Are you stupid? I wasn't working."

"We need the money."

"Then you should get out there. I'm tired of carrying your fucking ass. I'm not a whore."

"You giving your coño away to some pissant fuck in this neighborhood, then you dumber than any fucking whore out there."

"He loves me."

"Does he tell you that?"

"Fuck you."

"I'm your fucking mother."

"You've never acted like it."

"You're an ungrateful bitch."

"I'm my mother's child."

"If you don't work, you don't eat," she said. "We need the money."

Griselda stood up, the fury rising in her blood. "I'm done working," shouted Griselda.

"You're done working when I say you're done working."

"I'm done being some puta on the street. I'm done letting your asshole boyfriends fuck me because they can't fucking get any traction in your used-up ass." Griselda went over to a bag she had in the corner that she kept her clothing in and grabbed it. "I'm done with you!" She stared at her mother.

Suddenly, her mother's hand came across her face. Ana grabbed her daughter by the back of the head, yanking on a fistful of her hair, and pulling her to the ground, as Griselda screamed like a banshee.

Pain burrowed its way into Griselda's head as she pulled at her mother's hand. She slapped her mother in the face and her mother balled her hand into a fist and slammed it into Griselda's face.

Griselda kicked at her mother's leg, knocking her to the floor. The front of her shirt tore open and her breast came out of her shirt as her mother fell backwards, holding on to her shirt, and tearing it from her chest. This was her only chance. She had to go now or she was going to have to kill her mother or her mother was going to kill her.

Bleeding, crying, she got to her feet while her mother laid on the floor, struggling to get back up. Drunkenly searching for a bottle or something to throw at Griselda. And Griselda ran for the door. She burst out into a rainy night, lightning illuminating her breasts, as she ran from the shanty, her mother screeching behind her. "You never come back here! You never fucking come back here! I'll kill you. I'll kill you!"

She didn't stop running, going into the dark streets, mostly abandoned for the storms, because the streets flooded so goddamn often. The dirt had turned to mud and her feet sank deep into it as she kept running. Her hands tried her best to cover her breasts. But she had to get to Rafi. That was all that was on her mind. He'd take her in…

CHAPTER 3

1) 1959

Griselda layered a foundation around her eye, staring at her face in the mirror, at the swell beneath her cheek, and the blackish purplish bruise that she tenderly touched up. The door to the bathroom opened and she swallowed nervously as Rafi came in. "I didn't mean to hit you so hard," he said, wrapping his arms underneath hers, his forearms propping up her breasts. He kissed the top of her head and she couldn't help but feel warm and cared for.

"I didn't mean to get you angry. You know I'm jealous... you shouldn't have been flirting with that puta..."

"I wasn't flirting. I was putting on a show. If people think we're together... You know the drill." She knew he was lying, but it was easier to just go along with it. She wasn't crazy. But Griselda let him think she believed him and didn't call him on his bullshit.

"It's fine... I know..."

"You ready for tonight?"

"I'm getting there. Got to look presentable," she said with a coldness.

He craned his neck and kissed her cheek. Sliding his arms from her, he slapped her ass and grinned at her.

Clubs in the center of the Medellin came to life toward the end of the week, music boomed, and white businessmen, trying to do business in Colombia, hung out, drank, and sampled the women and drugs of their potential new land.

El Perro Loco had become their personal hunting ground. Markos did the books for the man that owned the club, and Jacko worked as an enforcer for the club owner in all his business dealing. Which gave them both the freedom to put people on the list. The owner only cared that a few people never got fucked over. But outside of a few high rollers that partook in the backroom activities of the club and their guests, the club owner had a laissez-fair attitude with what happened to the people that were spending their time treating the country like their personal playground.

Rafi dealt weed and cocaine and Griselda would then pickpocket their money... Jacko and Markos would then get their cuts. She wouldn't pickpocket everyone. That would be bad business and get them banned sooner than later. No, she saved that for special nights. Two to three times a month, when some rich white men would be showing off their money and just begging to be robbed. Other times, she played the seductress. She learned English just for the role. Broken English, but the Americans that came seemed to like that even more. She would hang on their arms. Talk in their ears, let them touch her, but always stop from getting too personal. Then tell them they should buy her drugs, drink more, until they would get completely wasted and she'd disappear. This was why the owner of the club didn't mind them coming around and didn't mind their occasional thefts of his clients.

On a good night, she could get men to buy up anywhere from fifty to one hundred dollars more of alcohol from the bar. She'd drink some, throw the rest, and leave them with a good experience of a fun night with a Latin "Chica."

One fun night, she got men to buy over a hundred and fifty dollars in weed and cocaine, and she kept giving it back to Rafi to just resell to her again and again and again. It was funny to her and it became a challenge for her to see how many times she could get guys to keep buying her the same weed or coke.

But it was the nights that she could steal that made all the money.

Griselda loved stealing, because outside of sex, it was one of the few things that she was great at. She was an artist when it came to picking someone's pocket. A bump for distraction, a slip of the hand, and before the person even knew what was happening, Griselda would disappear with their money shoved into her clothes. If pick-pocketing was an art form, Griselda was Picasso. She had an innate ability to know exactly when someone was perfectly distracted. She couldn't explain it. She couldn't put it to words. It was a feeling in the air, an intuition, a sensitivity to when the winds of change had brushed past a person. It wasn't just because of her light touch and slight frame, or the quickness of her feet to be long gone before they even questioned anything, but there was one other thing she was very good at, and that was disappearing.

And, more than anything, what made her different from most petty thieves that lurked around the clubs or the rowdy streets outside at night, is she could steal from someone, and by the time they looked around to figure out who touched them, she could change her look. Whether it was changing her wig before the person could even glimpse in her direction, flipping a coat, or stripping off a shirt for one underneath, she could make herself whatever she needed to make herself so good that she could sit down with someone the next day, after spending all night dancing with them, and they wouldn't recognize her one bit.

It was why she took her time to make sure she hid the black eye perfectly. That no one would notice that she had one, because something like that would make her stand out. It was something that people remembered. It was something that put people on a greater level of alert. And none of that was good for theft.

She took a wig, figuring to go blond and straight this evening, fitted it on her head, and then checked her lipstick in the mirror. She was, if she had to say so herself, perfect. She wasn't too beautiful, nothing more special than any of the other girls that were out there. She wasn't unattractive either, in any way that would draw attention. No. From her shapely body and tight black shirt and her own modified skirts that she sewed compartments into in order to sequester all the stolen goods and not have to juggle them in her hands, or put them in her bra or purse – which she'd seen plenty of thieves get them caught doing. With a mix of padding and buttons, in the less than the time for the person to pat their pocket, she could sequester away an item and even if they patted her down, they'd never find it. More importantly, she cultivated a very specific look. She was attractive enough to catch the eye when she wanted the attention and absolutely forgettable when she left. She made herself look like everyone else.

Tonight, Rafi was making his rounds, having left before her. This way, no one connected the two of them together and if anything went wrong for either of them, the other could do what they could to help without being implicated.

Rafi moved through the club with ease. Tall, handsome, dressed in a silk shirt, it was clear what he was, and no one hesitated to come up and buy from him. Jacko held for him, so he could re-up and never worry about having a lot of drugs on him. Twice guys had tried to jump him for the drugs, which both times he tossed and ran instead of staying and trying to fight, since it was only ever fifty to a hundred dollars' worth and he made that much in an hour or two. Besides, it was easier to get revenge later than it was to have to deal with people on their terms. He found one of the men that assaulted him, shot him in both his knees and left him in his house bleeding and unable to walk. The story went the man had to crawl himself outside and across the dirt road before he found someone to get him to a hospital. And by the time he got there, they had to amputate a leg. No one had tried to rob Rafi since.

When Griselda got to the club, she watched Rafi. Man by man coming up, pulling money out of one pocket or another, and then putting the rest of their money back. The white guys were shit with being discreet and the partiers were often too drunk to care – not that many of their own people had much money to steal. Them buying drugs took all the guesswork and luck out of stealing from them. It was like when she was young and would steal candy from the store. So easy a seven-year-old could do it.

Within an hour, she had a series of targets.

There were two white men in suits in their thirties, happy with the weed they could buy off Rafi, who got on the dance floor to see if any women were interested in going back up to their hotels and smoking with them.

Walking over to the bar, she barely even had to bump them. They were too distracted with the women that agreed to go on the dance floor with them, hoping that an American could steal them away from this life. Her hand slipped into one pocket and then, in a rhythmic spin and twist, into the other's pocket, and by the time she made it to the bar, she had their wallets in her skirt pockets. By the end of the night, she'd relieved five people of their wallets, their money-clips, and even a wedding ring that a man took off and had in his pocket. That was more for fun than profit, cause it didn't look that valuable.

Griselda smiled at Rafi as she was leaving. Knowing when to leave was just as important. Just because they didn't know who robbed them, once someone started taking notice that someone *had* robbed them, it would put everyone else on high alert. This left Rafi alone with drugs to sell and women to flirt with. It was the only thing she didn't like about their strategy.

At home, she waited for Rafi, so they could count out their haul. She hated when he was out there by himself, if only because sometimes he didn't find his way back to their apartment. Shacking up with some cunt that probably offered to suck his dick for some basuco or coke… coming back lousy after his roll with the pigs.

Turning on the radio, she lit herself a joint and stared impatiently at the door, waiting for him to return.

It wasn't until two in the morning, three hours after she left, that he came into the apartment. Stumbling, high, drunk, a mixture of the two. "How much more you sell?"

"Don't fucking worry about it," he grumbled.

"I'm just asking."

"How much did you get?" Rafi asked, as she laid out the haul of wallets and money clips on the table.

"Probably more than you," Griselda teased, trying to lighten the mood, and wanting to actually count out everything they made. They had plans, after all. Getting out of Medellin. Getting out of Colombia. Not ending up the way most thieves and dealers ended up in the country. Dead, in prison, or – steal from the wrong person – raped, tortured, and murdered... gender immaterial.

"Oh, really?" Rafi asked lightheartedly, the tenseness and bossiness disappearing in his voice. He came over to her and buried his face in her neck. She moaned as he sucked on the nape between her shoulder and neck, his hot breath warming her entire body from the cool darkness she was sitting in all night.

"Really," said Griselda, giggling like that little girl she once was those years ago. She grabbed for the money on the table, the discarded wallets in the trash, as she fanned the bills in front of his face.

Rafi lounged back against the couch, taking a deep breath, and letting the pleasure of the high flood him.

After Rafi's mother passed, they had moved out of the shanty and into a small brick apartment, still in the ghetto, but with a few more amenities than the shanty they were living in, and further from her mother, who she would continue to see around the neighborhood while they were there.

The apartment was gorgeous. It had real rooms and a real floor. There were lights and a bathroom and running water that they didn't have to boil to use. An indoor toilet and electric lighting. They were near a movie theater as well, which is where she spent most of her days when Rafi and she weren't hustling. She loved American films. The Wild Ones, Rebel Without A Cause, and the host of films that just kept making their way to their theaters. She had dragged Rafi to see Gone with the Wind a couple of times until he started balking at the suggestion.

"We did good today," Rafi said, sweeping the money from her hand and putting it into his pocket.

Griselda stared at him. She hated that he took all the money like it was his. "You know, I'd like some money too."

"How much do you want?"

"Half?"

Rafi laughed and pushed away from her on the couch. "Don't be stupid. Do I ever leave you wanting?"

"No," she said.

"Then what's the problem?"

Griselda and Rafi had this argument weekly, it felt like. What was the problem? She wasn't married to him. He was fucking other women. And she wasn't some fucking whore, being pimped out, not worthy of her own cash. That was just the thoughts off the top of her head. "I made the money too."

"We made the money," Rafi corrected.

"I'm just saying…"

"You're just saying what?" Rafi asked, annoyed. His eyes hardened as he glared at her. And she felt the coldness run through her spine.

Griselda went quiet. "Nothing…" she grunted. He grabbed the pipe and metal sheet and laid out some basuco to smoke. "Again…?" she asked.

"You smoke it as much as I fucking smoke it. Don't give me that," Rafi said.

"But we smoked already… when you do too much, it makes you paranoid."

"I don't get paranoid."

"Okay…"

"Okay?"

"Okay! I'm going to bed," Griselda said and stood up.

Rafi grabbed her arm and pulled her down to the couch. "Don't do that! I'm not some fucking addict. I make plenty of money. Keep you in some nice clothes. In this nice place. Off the fucking streets. So don't be a fucking ungrateful bitch."

"Fuck you!" she said, standing back up, her leg bumping the table as she did it, knocking over the basuco onto the floor. Watching it, it was like seeing it in slow motion. The thin sheet of metal hitting the floor with a clack that shook her entire body, as the powder scattered across the floor. "I'm sorry!" Griselda cried, jumping back from him, but unable to get far enough.

Rafi was up and throwing her against the wall before she could say anything else. He grabbed her by the throat, pinning her. "Why do you fucking do this?" he yelled in her face. His hand tightening on her throat.

"It was an accident. I'm sorry." Her voice squeaked out the words as she struggled to breathe.

"Sorry! Sorry!" His hand struck her across the face and she felt her jaw click and could taste blood in her mouth. "I took you out of the fucking ghetto. I got us making nice fucking money. I did all of this for us." His grip tightened as his words got angrier.

She pulled at his fingers, trying to get him to let go. "It... was... an... accident!"

With an angry toss, he threw her across the floor. Her leg scrapping across it. "Get in the fucking bedroom and shut your fucking mouth if you don't want to fucking smoke! I swear Griselda! Sometimes you just look for ways to piss me off."

She moved slowly, picking herself up off the floor, and going over to the bedroom, and opening the door, and crawling in. Sitting down on the comfortable mattress, she massaged her leg and rubbed her face, feeling the heat from his hit, while she listened to Rafi through the thin wall. Her jaw ached, her leg ached, and rage poured through her veins like molting metal, hardening everything inside of her.

Rafi had taken what was a casual thing they would do occasionally, fuck on a lot, and party on, into a full-blown habit. To where a huge percent of the money they were making was going to his habit. Sitting in the dark of the room, seeing the night sky through a window, and wanting more than this... Griselda felt that restlessness growing inside her. She had to go. This wasn't the place for her to make the life she truly wanted.

Rafi lumbered his way into the bedroom, tossing open the door. His pants off and his cock dangling between his legs Griselda lifted her head from her hands and stared at him. She felt nothing at that moment. Nothing for him. Nothing about the situation.

He stomped forward with heavy feet falling loudly on the floor. "Let's make-up!" Rafi said, the buzz from the basuco running through his system.

When Rafi was asleep and the sun was up, Griselda got dressed quietly and went over to the kitchen and grabbed a knife. She marveled at the tip of the blade. The shininess of the metal. The sharpness of the edge. He was passed out. Sleeping like a brick, like always. She could do it, she thought. Stab him through and disappear. It wasn't like anyone was going to investigate the death of some drug dealer in an apartment. Hell, spill a little basuco on the floor, a little weed here and there, and it would just be another dead dealer who got his from some junkie.

The thought of it didn't scare her nearly as much as she thought it would. It had been years since she had killed Alex, nearly seven years, and except for the first few nights, she had lost little sleep over it. Griselda looked at the door, hearing Rafi snort and go back to snoring. The knife tightened in her grasp.

But he was Rafi. He was her first love. He got her away from her mother. Got her away from the slums. He wasn't some rich kid who had everything and deserved whatever happened to him because he was weak.

But she couldn't stay. No.

She knew she couldn't stay any longer.

No matter what she did.

Kill him or let him live.

She couldn't stay.

Keeping the knife in hand, she walked over to the living room, and saw his pants casually laying on the floor. She bent down and picked them up and reached into the pocket and pulled out their haul from last night.

Griselda stared at the money. If she took it all, he'd come for her, no doubt. Search for her non-stop. Because if someone took her money, that's what she'd do. But half... Half was a message... a message that she wasn't going to be able to return, and if she did, there'd be pain waiting for her. But she could do something with half.

She counted out the money. It was a better-than-expected hall. Nearly three hundred American dollars. Those businessmen liked to walk around with cash. It was why they were such ideal targets. She counted out a hundred and fifty dollars between the pesos and dollars and shoved them into her pocket. She'd need new clothes. New wigs. New make-up... A new life... She decided to take another twenty. Hearing him shift about uncomfortably in the bed, snort once more so loud it sounded like the bedroom door was open, she knew it was now or never... Going was the only option... Go or kill him... or both... but the longer she kept thinking about it... Staying was never an option.

Griselda got up and put on her shoes and walked to the door. She stared at the apartment. Stared one last time at this life she didn't think she'd ever have. Was she crazy? She couldn't tell. Maybe she was. Or maybe the music had played its last song for her in this part of her life. Either way, she turned away from the apartment, patted the money in her pocket, and left.

PART 3
A DOMESTIC LIFE
CARLOS TRUJILLO

CHAPTER 4

1) 1959

Griselda ran her fingers through Gabriela's straight flowing hair before pulling her into a kiss. Beside them, two men sat, holding their crotches in one hand, hooting pleasantly, urging them to go further, do more, while tossing extra dollar bills at them, over what they already paid. This was, for Griselda and Gabriela, one of the more profitable ways of prostituting, away from the brothels.

Gabriela grabbed the hem of Griselda's shirt and pulled it over her head, revealing her naked back to the men and bare breasts to her. Her nipples hardened. She liked the feel of Gabriela's hands. She liked Gabriela's body. Griselda brought her mouth to Gabriela's breast, cupping the tender brown mound in the palm of her hand, and taking the dark nipple in between her teeth. The men went crazy. They always went crazy when she did that with Gabriela. They moved their chairs closer to the bed and Griselda felt a hand fall onto her ass from one of the men and she moaned for their pleasure, keeping her focus on Gabriela, and moving to the other breast.

Griselda kept telling herself that this time would be the last time. She'd said it several times before. But the money was just so good for these things. One session with some horny Americans or rich politically connected Colombians over here from Bogota, and she made rent and food for the month. She hated prostituting, but stealing was never as consistent, and the more she had to do, the more dangerous it became.

If not for Carlos, it wouldn't even be a concern for her. She really enjoyed doing things with Gabriela – about as much as Gabriela enjoyed doing stuff with her. But Griselda was seeing Carlos and she was starting to actually care for him, love him even, and it seemed like he was beginning to fall for her. Carlos was an older man, much older than Griselda, and knew her profession before he got involved with her. Her profession was the reason that they met in the first place. But the moment he fucked her, she became an obsession for him. And she liked him. He was smart. Ambitious. Traveled. And he had money. Not a huge amount. But he had money. He wanted her to quit, and she kept telling him that he would... but these opportunities kept coming up. What was a girl to do? It wasn't like he was paying her bills.

Gabriela tossed her head back, playing it up for the two businessmen that paid extra for the show. Griselda had found a taste for women that she didn't quite know she had until it happened. Growing up, she had always found other women attractive, Lydia being the first she had any feelings for, but it wasn't until she was back to working the streets and realized that men would pay a lot more to see two women together before fucking them, that she found a real passion for sleeping with women. Gabriela bent the same way and Gabriela had become more than a roommate for her.

Gabriela laid back on the bed and Griselda stuck her ass high in the air as she brought her mouth down to her panty clad pussy and put her mouth over the cotton material. "Oh yeah, chicas," one man moaned, getting up to get a perfect view of what Griselda's tongue was doing. Gabriela knew her role well and she brought her hand to his crotch and started rubbing him over the fabric and a look of ecstasy came across the man's face was like he had just taken the greatest drug ever made. Both men really went crazy. Screaming and hollering, clapping their hands, and starting to undress themselves. Bogota tourists, Americans working with the conservative government, just the overall growth in the economy as La Violencia was rumoring to be ending. It meant there were so many people slosh with money if you knew where to look, and Griselda was always determined to know where to look.

The man Gabriela was rubbing on came over to her head, pulling his pants down, and offering up his small member like it was some sort of grand prize. It bounced proudly and jerked in her hand as Gabriela grabbed it and guided it into her mouth. A moan burst from the man and she joined, as Griselda slid her panties to the side.

The two men paid a pretty penny for the show and then they were still showering them with extra singles for the fun of it. They were Americans; they were used to spending more money for pussy than what most were out there charging on the street. And they didn't blink at twenty dollars apiece, when the average girl went for five or ten dollars, depending on where you were. Even in the center of Medellin, fifteen would usually get you a girl for the entire night if you wanted it. And for Griselda, she just had that enticement to her. She knew how to dress up the role, play the part... wherever she was. She could plan with her fellow ladies of the night, taking shots, and laughing at the ridiculous men that came their way, or she could dress up, put on make-up and mingle with the powerful... realizing as she had quickly learned, that appearance was everything.

Even a whore could become a queen, in Griselda's mind, and nothing short of queendom was going to be acceptable to her.

Connections were power. More than anything, that's what she learned from Rafi. You just needed an in and the world was yours. For Griselda, that first in was Gabriela, who didn't even know what connections she had.

She met Gabriela at a bordello. It didn't take much for the two hundred dollars to run out. She was still doing well, thievery was profitable, but then someone – she was sure Rafi, though it could've been anyone – had broken into her apartment and stolen her jewelry and the money she hid in the bed. Faced with homelessness and starvation, it wasn't a hard choice; she liked sex and hated poverty. Selling sex was the easiest route.

Initially, she had taken a few customers on the street, but after nearly being strangled by one, stabbing him in the hand with the knife she carried with her everywhere to get away, she thought a bordello would be safer than working the streets. Gabriela took her under her wing, lent her some clothes, and though Griselda didn't need any help to attract guys, she let Gabriela show her how she did it from the curb, with nothing but a smile and a glance.

Griselda showed her the fun of basuco and her connections kept them all in weed and gave her a separate stream of income in providing drugs to the girls.

Griselda climbed herself up Gabriela's body and joined her in pleasuring the customer, before she heard the other guy stand up behind her, and she kissed herself back down Gabriela's stomach, and to between her thighs, pushing her own ass up in the air, to greet the guy with a pleasant view.

Their friendship started when Gabriela was having trouble with a John that was following her. The bordello offered some – some being the most minimal possible – protection for the girls that worked for them, but when they left, they were on their own. Gabriela didn't want to be alone and Griselda had no qualms in showing her violent side to men that didn't take the hint, pulling a knife on the man and threatening to cut off his balls if she saw him again. She went as far as buying a gun and teaching Gabriela how to shoot it if necessary, showing her, like Rafi showed her, that time when she was eleven and then later in life. After that, they were good friends. And when Griselda needed a place to stay, Gabriela was in need of a roommate.

The other man came up behind Griselda, pulling down her skirt and panties, and she moaned into Gabriela's sex, as she wiggled her ass invitingly at the man behind her. She felt his hands seize her hips and he drove himself inside of her. She gasped and moaned louder, even though it wasn't nearly as big or powerful as she was making it seem.

Gabriela was beautiful in a way that Griselda never appreciated a woman's beauty before. Funny in a way that Griselda would usually find annoying, but didn't with her. And she didn't know when it transitioned to something more, but she knew when Gabriela approached her about clients willing to shell out twenty-five for the both of them to put on a show together, she was perfectly fine taking the money and having fun with Gabriela. And when Griselda realized that there was a market for such fun... she started to figure out how to capitalize on it.

The men came quickly, eventually taking both of them side by side. It was less than hour work and they had pocketed as much money as most people made in a week or where Griselda came from in a month, if they were lucky.

They left the room, pocketing the money in their purse, laughing at the fun and at the ridiculousness of the men, before getting into a beaten-up Renault and driving home. "I don't know how you find these guys, but goddamn if I don't love when you do!" Gabriela yelled proudly, kissing Griselda on the cheek.

"Just don't tell Carlos about it," said Griselda.

"No, we wouldn't want to do that, would we?" Gabriela laughed.

2)

"If you're going to be with me, you've got to be with me. You're lucky I'm not a jealous man and know a woman needs to make money, or I might be unpleasant," Carlos said to Griselda. There was a casualness to him, a calm that she liked and rarely experienced in the men she met. He handed her the joint and got out of bed and put his pants back on. He was in decent shape for a man in his late thirties, nearly forty. And she enjoyed fucking him. She liked that he always brought weed and that he talked about the places that he traveled to.

"It was good money, Zulma," she teased him, knowing he didn't like that name. He shot her a glare... "Carlos, it's not like you're being monogamous either.

76

You think I don't know when you fuck bitches? Desperate fucking hoes who want you to do their paperwork for free, throwing themselves at you." She rolled from the bed, wearing nothing but a long shirt he hadn't cared to take off when he fucked her. The material hung down to her knees and worked as a gown. She got on her knees in front of him, grabbing at his brown slacks that he just pulled up. "Please Carlos, anything Carlos, I'll suck your big thick cock... let you stick it in my culo... Just please. I fucking know when you fuck bitches, Carlos. At least I have a fucking reason. Besides... you enjoy it when Gabriela comes along to play as well."

Carlos laughed and leaned down and took the joint out of her mouth. He sucked on the tip, staring down at her, amused, as he puffed a cloud into the air above her head, and said, "I don't mix business and pussy. That's all I'm saying."

Looking up at him, her brown eyes big and full, "You want me?"

Her hand brushed his crotch. "I think I made that clear."

"You wanna take care of me, Carlos?"

He rubbed her hair like she was his pet, then tightened his hand, twisting her head so she stared directly at him. Carlos knew exactly how she liked it. He understood her body. Took time to learn it. The sensation rushed through her body, a shiver like a stiff breeze up her spine, and she bit her bottom lip and smiled. "I want you to be mine and only mine."

Griselda stood up, pressed against his body, his hand still in her hair. "You're so much older than me, Carlos," she said, offering a teasing glance. "I'm a lot to handle."

"I think I've shown that I can handle you."

"You think so?"

"You won't have to work with any of the shit you do now. I'll teach you to forge documents. You work with me. We make money. You'll be mine..." It was what she was waiting for. A real ticket out of this life. A ticket to a better life, a better... place, just better. And as she stared at Carlos, the gray slightly forming at the roots of his hair and around the side of his jawline, she still thought of him as a handsome man. Though admittedly, he was slightly balding. Age didn't matter to her. She'd been with men of all ages. Carlos had traveled the world, and most importantly, been to America.

America for Griselda was a dream, the only place where someone like her could escape from what her life had become. It had immediately made Carlos more attractive than ever before. He wasn't some easily duped businessman. He was like her. Grew up poor, if not the slums, then close to it. His father was murdered when he was a boy. He lived with his grandparents and mother and she had multiple other children. Considered smart by his teachers, often, he was labeled as too smart for his own good. He excelled at school, though it often bored him. And at sixteen, he left home when he realized he could make more money selling drugs, then any of the jobs his mother or grandparents worked, and more money than any of the teachers that taught him.

For years he made money moving weed and cocaine and basuco on the streets. He dabbled in heroin, but didn't like the clientele. He built a network of people, kept his nose dry, not partaking in the drugs himself, except for a little pot here and there. Partially for self-preservation, partially because it interested him, he started forging documents in his spare time. It was easy money when you could get it done right, safer than drugs. When he had to get one of his friends out of the country, people heard how quickly and easily it was for his friend to get out and go to America that soon he was swarmed with requests. And outside of selling some weed through a few dealers of his own, he spent his time document forging.

For Griselda, that was the big draw. When Carlos told Griselda that he had just come back from America, the third time he had hired her services, she was instantly full of questions. Where did he go? What did he do there? Was it a onetime thing, or did he do it more? They talked all night about America and, by the end, she didn't charge him a dime.

They started dating, as much as a hooker can date her John. In this weird and quasi way, both aware the other wasn't loyal, nor intended to be loyal, and yet, it felt like one of the best relationships she'd ever had. She loved learning of his mind. Of how forging documents works.

"You really want me to be yours?" she asked, charmed. She had been maneuvering for this for a while. Teasing him. Playing with him. Going cold and then hot. Showing him the pieces of herself that she often tried to keep hidden. Every action. Every bit of information she let him know. All of it was to shape just this desire in him. She wanted to be his. To be his wife. To be taken out of this world. It was the hope of most of the girls she worked with – except for those who had long become jaded with the prospect of love and liked their freedom and their habits.

"I really want you to be mine," said Carlos.

Griselda took Carlos's hand that was holding the joint between his fingers and brought it to her mouth and she puffed on it, until the embers retreated to his fingers, and he pulled it from her mouth. "What do you want from me?"

He grabbed her and turned her around, pushing her across the bed. If there was one thing that made Carlos stand out was his endurance. He fucked like the rich made money, always wanting more. He pushed up her nightgown and kicked open her feet. "I want you to quit all this fucking foolishness. Be my woman. And only my woman!" He emphasized the last bit by slamming himself inside of her and she moaned. "I want you to have my kids. I want you to be my wife. I want... I want... I want you!" Carlos moaned before enveloping himself in a rhythm.

3) 1962

Griselda screamed so loud her throat burned.

She wondered if she would have thought twice about it if she knew this was what being his would lead to. They'd married five months ago and she was already having his child.

She already resented him a little. Not so much for the pregnancy, but because they hadn't yet been to America. He had gone for business, smuggling people out of the country, as he did. But Griselda remained home, in their house, in a place she never thought she'd be. Barefoot and pregnant and wondering if she made the right choice.

Her legs in stirrups, a doctor telling her it was all going to be okay, that she was doing good.

Carlos sat in the waiting room, excited, waiting to hear about the birth of his son. He knew it was going to be a boy. Trujillos were known for their strong line of men. He sucked on a cigarette, stubbing one out, and replacing it with another in an ashtray beside him. Dressed in a leisure suit, looking around and sipping whiskey from a flask, while he heard his wife scream from the delivery room. "I should've never married him!" Griselda yelled. "Ah fucking hell!" she screamed. He rolled his eyes, unfazed by her complaints. He suspected something she'd be like this. Was actually surprised that she wasn't in more foul a mood. Horny as hell, though, those were some fun active months.

Drinking more, he relaxed and waited.

Watching as the head crowned, the doctor told her, "Push Griselda, he's almost out, push..." And she bared down once more and felt an excruciating pain shoot through her body. Sweat soaked her gown to her breasts as she heaved breathy gasps, trying to rein in the dull throbbing between her thighs. "One more push," they said again. That's all they kept saying. "One more push." But that was three pushes ago, and she wasn't sure she could push anymore. Tears were exploding from her eyes as she felt the final release. The baby, her baby, pulled from between her thighs, and a moment of relief pour through her body as the baby screamed to life and the doctor held it up.

"Es un niño," the doctor said, taking the baby and bringing it over to Griselda and putting it in her arms. He was already a handsome little boy. She stared at his small narrow face and the sticky dark matte of hair on his head and he looked so much like his father. Nurses went out and came back in with Carlos in tow. Carlos took another swig from his flask and stubbed out his cigarette in a pan the nurses held out for him. He came over and stared at the boy.

"I'll trade you," he said, holding out the flask, and reaching for his son.

Griselda was happy for the exchange, taking the flask in one hand, and carefully handing the baby off to Carlos in another. She drank hungrily for the pain, wanting anything to dull the throbbing between her legs. She was wondering if she'd ever even have sex again, let alone have another child. But looking at Carlos, as he rocked his baby in his arms, her mind was quickly changing. Carlos waved a finger above the baby's closed eyes, touching his tiny nose, while he cradled him in his arm. His eyes were a bit glassy, but she couldn't hold that against him.

Griselda was happy that Carlos was happy. She was happy to be a mom. Most of all, she was happy the birth was over. She stared at her husband and her son, as the doctors left the room for a minute for the two of them to be alone. She'd come so far. Gotten so much. Had a life she couldn't imagine.

Carlos sniffed back a tear and rubbed his face against his shoulder to catch it before it rolled down his cheek. Griselda smiled. Staring at him, Griselda couldn't help but remember why she fell in love with the man in the first place. That tenderness. That care.

"Dixon," said Carlos, running his finger down the baby's nose. "Little Dixon. Mi nino!"

4) 1964

Griselda was cooking empanadas. She was sweating, even under the two fans she had blowing on her. She was sipping ice water, taking ice cubes underneath her tongue, trying to keep herself calm and cool. Dixon ran around the house with a toy plane, making "whoosh" sounds, as his two-year-old legs pumped like a locomotive, unable to be stopped. "Mama, mama, look at me," he said.

"I see, I see you," said Griselda. Her stomach swelled outward, but her feet felt much more swollen. She was having a hard time this morning. Her stomach felt overburden, just off. It wasn't painful. She was sure she still had a couple of weeks left until the baby was to arrive. So she wasn't thinking about the baby coming. It couldn't be that. Whatever it was, though, it was making her feel short with everything and everyone.

Dixon kept whooshing about, making gun turret sounds, "Choom, Choom, Boom, POW!" He was enjoying himself. Then he bumped her right as she was picking the pan off the stove. She dropped it back on the stove, and grease splattered on her hand. Pain seared across the top of her hand as she gritted her teeth and tried to shake the grease off of it. "Fucking hell!" she snapped. "Go in the living room! Or sit down!" she yelled!

Dixon's face dropped and he stared at Griselda before puckering a shivering lip, his eyes filling with tears, and his little nose twitching as he took sharp breaths, trying to fight back the urge to cry. Then, once the dam broke and everything flooded from his eyes, she went to the sink and ran her hand underneath the cold water, while Dixon ran himself into the living room and tossed himself onto the couch. He bawled loudly, and she felt horrible for it. She hated hearing him cry.

Griselda grunted and gritted her teeth, trying to calm herself down, as she scooped the empanadas from the grease.

She didn't think this was what life was going to be like. She had bigger dreams than being some kept woman. Bigger goals than being a soon-to-be mother of two. Not that she didn't love Dixon. Not that she wasn't excited about the baby on the way. Just that she still wanted more. Needed more than a house and television. Yes, she was living in luxury compared to how she had growing up. But every night, as she went to sleep, the feeling was there, the call, the nibble of dreaded disappointment, that this couldn't be all there was. There had to be more.

After she got the empanadas on a napkin to get the excess grease off them, she wandered into the living room, with Dixon, burying his face in a pillow, his toy plane thrown in the corner. "I'm sorry, niño," she said. "Mommy burnt her hand and she got angry. You know how you get when you scrape a leg, or thump a toe, right?" She showed her burnt hand.

"Do you want me to kiss it?" Dixon asked.

"Very much so," she said, offering her hand to his lips. The coolness of his mouth added to the sting, but she smiled anyway.

"There, does that make it better?" he asked.

"Si, very much so. In fact, your kisses, I think, are going to be my medicine for all my ailments. If I got a toothache, I'll take a kiss here," she turned her head and pointed to her cheek, and he kissed it and smiled. "If I have a headache…" She lowered her head and he kissed her forehead. "You're a good boy, Dixon. Mama's sorry for yelling."

Dixon was looking more and more like his father, in his younger years, when he still had a full head of hair (in the few pictures Griselda had seen of him in his younger time). From his round face, to his black hair, and his troublemaking, he was Carlos's child, no doubt.

Rambunctious and industrious like his father, smart and creative like his mother, and always getting into trouble like the both of them. The moment he learned to walk, he ran, with little care, if he fell on his face. He barely cried. But boy was he a handful. Whether it was nearly setting the house on fire when he turned on the stove. Or it was getting trapped under the house when he decided to see what was beneath their ramshackle home. Griselda felt blessed that there weren't any snakes under there that day or he would've been a dead little niño. She couldn't imagine what a second one was going to be like. She really thought Dixon was enough.

Griselda stood from the floor and made her way back to the kitchen, Dixon getting up and following her, when suddenly a pang of discomfort grabbed at her stomach. She bent forward, grabbing her stomach, moaning, as suddenly she felt water pouring down her legs.

Dixon started to shout. "Mommy pee peed! Mommy pee peed!" The coldness settled around her bare feet and on her inner thighs. Shit, she thought to herself, Carlos wasn't here.

She stared down at the mess and sighed. Griselda wanted to be happy, but she couldn't stop thinking about how she told Carlos never again. But a night of drinking, a little basuco, and suddenly he was forgetting to pull out, and nine months later, here she was, the size of a small whale. Her poor feet. They didn't swell nearly as bad when she was pregnant with Dixon, but now, she could barely put shoes on. Her face was round and fat. Her breasts aching and hard with milk. And Dixon... Dixon... her angelic monster... getting on her nerves yelling, "Fat mama, fat mama!" because he heard Carlos say it playfully one night.

It was happening now. Carlos wasn't even going to be here for it – not that he'd been here much in the raising of the kids. Just working more and more, running another puta to the United States, even when she told him to stay. She was annoyed. Annoyed that she was going to have another kid. Annoyed with Carlos, who seemed to just use it as an opportunity to "work" more, which she was certain meant fuck around with those desperate bitches she once mocked him for. Annoyed.

Carlos wasn't helping matters. He ignored her accusations, of course, as he always did. But in that cruel, gaslighting way. "Really? Is that what you think? Wasn't it you that was fucking other men while we were dating? Wasn't it you that fucked around on people? Are you sure you're not just feeling guilty yourself? You spend a lot of nights alone," he'd accuse her. But they always made up. They always apologized. And she was willing to give him the benefit of the doubt, even though she was sure he probably got some sort of favors from a few desperate bitches. But it could all just be the pregnancy brain, she hoped.

"Dixon!" she yelled, as she straightened herself up and caught her breath.

He stopped once more, standing straight, unsure how to respond.

"We got to go!" she said.

"Go mama? Go where?"

"Just come here Dixon!" she yelled and once more the boy began to tear up and cry.

She tossed the apron on the floor over the spill of her broken water. She bent over with difficulty and grabbed Dixon, tearful and heavy, off the floor and into her arms, and hauled him through the door and to their car. She tossed him into the backseat and moved to the driver's seat as pain clenched her abdomen and snatched around into her lower back and she moaned, clenching so tight into the door that she lost feeling in her fingers. Tears burst into her eyes and she ground her teeth, breathing through her nose, and trying to calm her body down. She could do this. She had to do this.

Why did Carlos have to work so close to the baby's arrival? She had a bunch of thoughts going through her head as she threw herself into the car with a determinate locked jaw. She shoved the key into the ignition and the engine didn't turn over. She tried again. And no luck. She tried again, pumping the gas, saying a prayer, and turning the key so hard she thought it would snap in the ignition. The engine hiccupped and burped and came to life and she sighed with a painful moan as she hit the gas and headed for the hospital.

Uber was born silent. He wasn't moving. He wasn't squirming. He wasn't like Dixon at all. "Is he okay?" she asked, sitting up in the bed, even as her whole body hurt.

The doctors didn't answer her. They pulled him aside and they examined him while Griselda looked on worriedly. "Is he okay?" she whispered hoarsely, her throat raw, and her body so painfully sore, she didn't want to move.

Dixon was being watched by a nurse.

There was no calling Carlos, because his line of work required him not to leave a trail that was easily traced or reachable. Not that he could run home in the middle of a job anyway.

She watched on as doctors huddled around her son, and a frenzy of activity started happening. One doctor reached for an instrument; a nurse handed some sort of mask. There was movement everywhere. Everywhere. They cleared Uber's breathing pathway. They listened to his chest. And they rubbed his chest until he made a hiccup sound and began squirming ever so slightly. His voice came to life. A cry and a cheerful air of relief circled through the nurses and the doctor. Griselda's heart fluttered in relief as well. As much as she was uncertain of having another child. Seeing him changed her mind immediately. It was all worth it, she thought. Even if life wasn't what she wanted it to be. Uber was still worth it.

A nurse brought Uber over to Griselda and she looked at the little baby with his misshapen head and dark eyes and held him close to her chest. He looked a lot like her, though his head needed time for him to grow into, and his nose was flatter. She held him close to her breast. "Hola, Uber, yo soy tu madre," she said.

He squirmed and he reached and Griselda was okay with it... With all of it... For now... She had to be... For Uber... For Dixon.

5) 1967

"Got you," said Dixon, seizing his little brother in a headlock. Uber let out a scream that made Griselda miss when he was a quiet baby. "Stop trying to steal my stuff!" Dixon yelled.

"Mama!" Uber yelled. "Mama!"

Griselda moaned, staring at her television, her feet resting in the cold water, while she sipped on some weed to help with the nausea. She took her feet from the pool of water and dried them on a towel beside the bucket and she stood up, her stomach once more stretched and pushing out. Her eye was swollen, which she had told Dixon and Uber was because she accidentally ran into a cabinet, but it was the usual fights she was having with Carlos and his penchant of late to throw a fist whenever he was frustrated.

She didn't even remember what this fight was about. His drinking. Never taking them to America, like he had promised so many times. To him, he said, "America is work. I take you to Salenta, Guatape, Jardin, or Jericho, all more beautiful and better than America. Safer too. We don't want to be busted just for being tourists."

Griselda didn't know what to say. She didn't know why she stayed. "Momma!" Uber cried and she knew that was one of the reasons.

"He keeps trying to steal my stuff. It's my marbles and he keeps trying to take them because he loses his!" Dixon yelled in defense before Griselda could even inquire about what was happening.

Uber ran to his mother, wrapping himself around her leg, disappearing beneath her large pregnant belly, and craning his neck around it to find her face as she looked down at him. She loved how much Uber relied on her. He was so much a momma's boy, not at all like Dixon, who had a strong independent streak. He rarely ever came running to her or his dad. It was something Griselda admired in him, as much as she wished he wasn't like that.

"Don't beat up your brother," she said.

"He was stealing my marbles."

"I don't care. Don't beat up your brother!"

"You always take the baby's side," he huffed, tossing himself on his bed.

"I'm not a baby!" protested Uber, stomping his feet on the floor. "Mama, I'm not a baby. Tell him I'm not a baby!"

She rubbed his shaggy brown hair that was so much like hers. "You're not a baby. We'll buy you more marbles when I go back out, okay? Just let your brother have his."

"Why does he get new marbles? He's just going to lose them."

"While if you let him use yours and he loses them, you would get new marbles too."

"That's not fair."

"Life's not fair!" she shot back at him.

He huffed again and hugged himself and rolled his eyes. "I hate you!"

"You what?" Griselda asked, her voice low and threatening.

"I hate you! I hate you! I HATE YOU!"

"Uber, go get mama's slipper!" Griselda said, pushing Uber to the side.

Uber ran in his little waddle-like way into the living room of their home and grabbed her flat slipper with the hard sole from the floor and brought it to her.

Dixon didn't run, not like Uber would try to do. He didn't beg and plead, unlike Uber. "Get across the bed!" she said.

He glared at her, but got up and turned around and leaned across his bed, a frown on his face, but resigned to his punishment. Just as she lifted the slipper into the air above her head, however, she felt it again, that note of pain that surged through her stomach and into her back, and she knew it was coming to be that time again. She dropped the slipper and wandered outside to Carlos working on the car.

"Is it able to drive?" she asked.

"Almost. I'll be done in a little," he huffed, grabbing his flask and taking a sip.

"I don't think we're going to have a little, Carlos. I think we need it working right now!"

Carlos looked at Griselda and stared at her red face and her wide stance and the pained look that was on her face. "Oh," said Carlos. "I'll get the neighbor's car. You get the boys."

Carlos ran over to their neighbor's house and Griselda moved as quickly as she could, holding her stomach, and yelling for the boys to put on their shoes and come outside.

She grabbed her shoes and slid them on her feet. She grabbed Uber and Dixon and ran them out of the house and into the yard as Carlos pulled up in an old jalopy, its engine backfiring as the car idled, and he waited for her to get in.

He leaned forward, pulling the seat with him, to toss the boys in the back, and she went over to the passenger side. "Is this even going to make it to the hospital?"

"Don't start right now. It's the best I could get. Not many people even have cars in this neighborhood."

"If you made more money, that wouldn't be a problem."

"If you didn't have such a smart mouth, you wouldn't have that black eye," he retorted back.

"Just get me to the hospital, Carlos," she retorted.

Osvaldo was a normal baby, screaming to life the moment he was born. Carlos was with the boys, drinking, and likely getting to where he was going to pass out, which had become a common thing for him lately. Another thing they fought about often. If not that, then money, since his forging business was slowing down, and his drug dealing was almost non-existent. He wasn't turning out to be the industrious man she fell in love with those years ago who promised her those trips and adventures and she resented him for that. She resented having his babies. She resented being his.

She took Osvaldo from the nurse and held him for the first time, rocked him in her arms, and knew, in that moment, when she didn't want to share Osvaldo with him, didn't want the nurse to get her husband, that she was done with Carlos Trujillo. If not immediately, then when she could find something else, or someone else.

She wasn't going to tell him that.

No.

The only thing Griselda had to say to Carlos, when the nurse brought him and the kids into the room, was the simple, straightforward statement. She'd said it two other times… But this time, this time, she meant it. "I'm not having any more kids," she told him.

Their boys were tuckered out after spending six hours in the hospital. They curled themselves up like puppies in the chairs and were fast trying to get some sleep.

Carlos swigged from his flask and huffed back a derisive snort. "Good," he slurred. "Can't afford another fucking one if we wanted one. I should've had them plug you up after Dixon."

"Or maybe I should've cut it off," Griselda said.

"The fuck you say?" Carlos questioned.

"I'll go back on birth control."

"That's what I thought you fucking said," he slurred at her.

"Yeah, I'll do that," she said with a bitterness that bit at the back of her throat. Carlos glared at her and she glared back while she held little Osvaldo in her arms. He didn't even stir. If anything, he seemed to get more comfortable as they got angrier. He buried himself into her breast and she held him close to her heart, letting herself relax, calm down... think.

How could she get a new life?

6) 1968

Philipe Anwar sat in a bar, drinking a beer, while he made eyes at a woman he was pretty sure was a hooker across the bar. He was a tall man, skinny, with round glasses, and slick back hair. Dressed in tight clothes, the woman across the bar smoked a cigarette from a plastic stem. "Watch it asshole," said Philipe Anwar, after a stranger bumped into him. He pushed away from the bar, standing as a puddle of beer poured down his lap. "You fucking spilled my beer."

"Que?" asked the man. "Fuck off, puta. Go change your fucking pants or something, before you get yourself hurt."

"What the fuck you say to me, hijo de puta?"

"The fuck you call me, pirobo?"

Philipe shoved the man. The man responded with a right hook. Philipe's jaw clacked and stars danced in his eyes for a second before he got his balance back. He drove a fist into the man's stomach, causing him to pitch forward in pain, and then he followed it with a punch of his own across the man's face. The man fell to the ground and Philipe proceeded to kick him, again, and again in the stomach and ribs, yelling all the while, "You fucking pirobo. You try to fuck with me, motherfucker. You can't fuck with me. You don't even know who the fuck I am. I'm Philipe Anwar." Philipe kicked him twice more for good measure. Blood spurt from the man's mouth. And Philipe backed away.

He turned to the bartender, feeling a sense of pride at his accomplishment. His jaw still aching. And he said, "Give me a shot of whiskey, before I get out of here. Put it on this puta's tab."

His back was turned as he watched his drink being poured. His lips curved in a pleasant smile at the woman that was still looking oh so delicious at the end of the bar. "You want to get out of here, sweetheart?"

The woman finished her drink, but before she could respond, her eyes widened, and her mouth opened to say something. But before the words left her mouth, a gunshot erupted, and Philipe Anwar's brains spread across the bar and over on the glass, killing him before his body even hit the ground.

The man, just a man, who no one would really remember, and the police wouldn't put up a great effort to find, stood over Philipe, staring at the craterous hole that he put into Philipe's head. He took aim again. "Who's the pirobo now, puta?" He pulled the trigger again and the body jerked. People stared in shock, terror, and the man pocketed his gun like it was a normal day, and walked from the bar without as much as a word.

Philipe didn't even know what happened. One moment he was alive, another he was dead. A common occurrence for people in Colombia, especially in the drug trade, but over a beer? If he had been alive and heard about this happening to someone else, he would've thought, "What a fucking idiot to get yourself killed over a goddamn beer!" He would've laughed to himself and kept walking without another thought. But he was dead. And his business was dead with him.

7)

"Hola Chica, you are looking good," Griselda sang out, seeing Gabriela after nearly eight years. Standing up from the table at the restaurant, she walked around, smiling, her arms open, taking Gabriela in and pulling her close. She still smelled amazing as well.

Gabriela was still beautiful. Still thin. Her breasts were still perky. Her hips were still narrow. Gorgeous. It was clear, Griselda thought, that she hadn't had kids. But Griselda expected nothing less from Gabriella. Though for Griselda, she felt like she was getting puffy, her hair curled but feeling forever unkempt, her breasts – don't even get her started on her breasts. Her niño's drained her dry of every last drop. Gabriela still exuded that gorgeous energy that made her oh so attractive and fun to play with. Griselda wasn't sure she even knew what that energy was anymore. When it came to Carlos, the need to be anything more than a warm, wet hole for fifteen minutes was just doing unnecessary things. "You look beautiful too," said Gabriela.

"You don't have to lie," said Griselda smirkingly.

They sat at the table, exchanging pleasant looks in silence, not wanting to get right to business, even though they both knew that's why they were meeting.

Carlos's supplier, Philipe Anwar, did something very inconvenient by getting his head blown off by some drunk in the bar that he stupidly started a fight with. Supposedly, it was all over a spilled beer. Now, usually people getting themselves killed wasn't a big deal to anyone. Losing people was pretty common on the low-end sides of Colombian society. But, without his supplier, that meant Carlos' weed business was drying up. That meant that he was making less and less money. And things were hard as it is. He needed another supplier and Griselda needed to make more money to finally be rid of Carlos permanently.

The best place to start looking for help is your own network. That's what life had taught Griselda, even when most of her networks were shit. She still had one friend. She never lost touch with Gabriela, sending her pictures of her babies, and exchanging letters, happy for her friend when she told her she was getting out of the life for a man like Griselda did. Gabriela found her own gangster boyfriend to run away with. A man by the name of Jose Grio. For Gabriela, it wasn't so much love at first sight, as it was that she preferred packaging drugs and helping him move them much more than she did fucking men for money. He had a bad basuco habit and he barely ever fucked or got it up, which Gabriela enjoyed.

"How have you been?" Griselda asked.

"I've been good. Very good. Making money. Enjoying life. How old are your boys?"

"Dixon is five, nearly six. Uber's four. And Osvaldo is one."

"I never would've thought you'd have kids. Mommy Griselda. Just doesn't seem to have a ring to it."

"They are the wind beneath my wings."

"How 'bout Carlos?"

"The spit in my face."

Gabriela nodded understandingly, bringing her hand out and laying it on top of Griselda's. "He at least got you out of the life and got you some beautiful sons. Which is surprising given the look of him. You worry they're going to get his hairline."

"I hope they take after their mother."

"They are beautiful like her," said Gabriela.

"Gracias."

"So why'd you want to meet?"

"Business…"

"Disappointing," said Gabriela, pulling her hand away.

"I'm not saying pleasure is off the table," Griselda proffered flirtatiously.

Gabriela laughed softly. "What type of business?"

"I need a weed supplier and I was hoping you knew someone or you know, Jose knew someone."

"You were hoping that we knew someone?"

"That you had a supplier you could put me in contact with."

"Our guy moves a lot of product."

"I'm sure I can find a way to make it work."

"You're putting me in a spot," said Gabriela, running her fingers through her dark hair. "I want to help you."

"I don't want to get you in trouble. I'd never risk your life."

"It's not that. It's just…"

"What?"

"I don't want to insult you."

"You won't."

"Carlos' business isn't exactly… you know… known… he's moving a couple pounds a month. I don't want to waste his time and I don't want to waste yours."

"I'm telling you; Carlos isn't going to be the one running it this time. I need to get it to where it's making money. I need to start making money. And I'm looking to bring in some serious cash. Mucho dinero."

"I can't make any promises. You know. The man likes to keep a low profile. Doesn't like to hang his business out there. If he says okay, I'll give you his name and tell you where to meet him. But I can't promise that it'll go the way you want it to go. One… He'll probably see you… because you have assets that will interest him… but I don't see him talking to Carlos," said Gabriela. "I can vouch for you. Jose will vouch for you."

"You setting me up to fuck some guy?" Griselda asked.

"Only if you want to," said Gabriela. "And to be up front… you might fucking want to."

"Is he any good looking?"

"He's definitely not bad to look at."

Griselda giggled.

She wanted more money. She needed more money. It had been a year since she had decided to leave Carlos, and she was still with him. She wasn't going to leave her sons with him and she wasn't going to subject her sons to poverty.

At one point, when she first met Carlos, she thought she wanted her sons to be just like him, but now, she wanted them to be anything but like him. "Set it up. And do you think you have any dresses I could wear?"

8)

The club was full. People in front sat around tables with friends, watching the stage, as they dragged on cigarettes and enjoyed the music and fine alcohol and appetizers. Griselda was given basic instructions on what to look for. A semi good looking man, slick back hair, fashionable, but not garish, sitting in the back of the restaurant.

On stage, a man played guitar, strumming it with that rare Latin skill that made the women in front want to know what else he could do with his hands. A band soon joined in and people cheered when the man began to sing.

Griselda's focus was elsewhere. She walked to the back of the club, looking at the range of people that were there, trying to find someone that matched the description. She dressed in one of Gabriela's looser dresses, though even having let it out some left it snuggly fit, and pressing out her booty and breasts sumptuously, taking eyes off her less than thin stomach, which was precisely what she wanted. She did up her hair, fixed her face, and felt like she was her old self again. Gorgeous, attractive, powerful...

SINGLE… maybe. A chameleon, able to make herself anything she needed for whatever was required.

Her eyes met a man in the corner. His brow furrowed and his lips rolled as he cocked his head one way, then the next. There was a casualness to his stare, neither luring her in nor rejecting her. Taking her in, like she was taking in everything. He was very good looking, with a full head of black hair and a tumbler of scotch in his hand. He wore a silk shirt and a gold watch on his wrist. It had to be him, she thought, and proceeded over to the front of his table. "You're Gabriela's girl?" he asked her, sitting up straight.

Griselda nodded. Though she could feel the hint of nervousness in her stomach, she thought it would be worse. It amazed her at how calm she actually was. It had been years since she had done anything like this. And yet it felt like settling into a pair of well-worn shoes. "Si."

"Si?"

"I'm Gabriela's girl. You're Alberto?"

The man stared at her mutely for a moment, his eyes running up and down her body, taking in every inch of her. His lip jerked up and he audibly sucked spit through his teeth. He shrugged. "Sit down," he said.

Griselda sat down across from him on the other side of the booth and he offered a low, amused laugh. "Why are you here?"

"We need a new supplier."

"We?"

"My partner and I."

"Your partner? Where are they?"

"Not here. Gabriela said that you wouldn't want someone else here."

"I like to know who I'm working with."

"You'll be working with me," Griselda said. "I'll be your point of contact."

"And who are you?"

"Griselda Blanco," she said.

Alberto leaned across the table, he cocked his head. "Who is Griselda Blanco?"

"A woman that will make you a lot of money," she said and smiled, fluttering her eyelashes. "This is my deal."

"And how is your business going right now?"

"Before our distributor got his head blown off… we were moving five to eight pounds a month."

"A month?"

"Si…."

Alberto grabbed his drink and gulped it down and started to make like he was getting up. "This isn't going to work, sorry."

Griselda quickly slid around the booth to his side and grabbed his arm. He stared down at her painted nails, holding onto his sleeve, her wide eyes staring at him. "Wait… why? I can make anything work."

"You're too small time," he said, pulling his hand free.

"I don't want to be," he said.

"Look, Gabriela might be a friend of yours, but I run a business not a charity. I'm not here to help the poor and downtrodden get out of their struggles. Why would Gabriela send you here? This isn't right for you and it's not profitable for me to take the risk. I move fifty pounds a week. I supply distributors. I'm not here supplying low rent dealers."

"I'm not a dealer. You really move fifty pounds a week?"

Alberto stared down at her. Whether it was the hunger in her eyes, or the slight dimple in her cheek, he shooed her over and sat back down beside her. "Yeah, I really move fifty pounds a week. I was hoping she was setting me up with someone that could move at least twenty-five pounds a month, if not fifty. I buy in fifty-pound lots. If I'm adding a new distributor, I need someone to at least take on half and then I can find another distributor for the other half. But ideally, I was hoping you were going to say fifty. Gabriela lied and said you were looking to step up in this game. It's, like I said, not worth the risk."

Griselda grabbed his wrist, held it tight, knowing she would not get a second chance at this. "I want to move fifty pounds. Tell me how to do it. How would you do it?"

"I'm not a college," he said. "Why would I help you?" He tried to pull his arm away from her, but she held tight.

Griselda bit her lower lip. She pulled on Alberto's hand and slid it under her dress and to her panty covered crotch. The tips of his fingers stayed in the warmth between her thighs and he grinned at her before sliding his hand free. He smelled his fingers. "You can help me, because we can have a very profitable and rewarding relationship."

Alberto pushed the hair back from Griselda's eyes. "What do you want to know?"

"What would be needed to move that much?"

"Territory, packaging, and dealers… it's like any business. You build the right infrastructure, get in the right locations, have the right people in place, so that product moves safely and the money flows in. When you're dealing in drugs, there's a certain amount of violence that you have to do, making sure people actually are doing what they're supposed to do. That's the only difference."

"I can move fifty pounds," said Griselda.

Alberto laughed. "No, you can't," he said.

"I can get something going that can do that."

"If you could, you would've already. Besides, you're just the middle person. It's your husband right that you're buying for? Your husband, that's your partner?"

Griselda looked away. "My husband doesn't know what he's doing," Griselda said. "With a lot of things." She stared directly into Alberto's eyes and could see the smirk dance across his lips. "I can make it happen."

"You'll end up in jail."

"I've been a criminal since I was a eleven years old. Never been arrested yet." She rubbed her hand over his chest, while her other hand found his pocket. She pulled his wallet free, showing it to him and giving it back to him.

"Do you think being a thief makes me feel more comfortable selling to you?"

"I'm sure I can figure out a way to make you more comfortable with the arrangement. What do I need to do?"

Alberto Bravo laughed and brought his attention to the music playing. He signaled to the waitress to bring him the check and pulled a cash clip from his inner pocket, and laid down a hefty amount for the drink and a tip for the woman. "Let's get out of here and we'll talk some place quieter."

Griselda smiled. She nodded and followed him from the booth.

CHAPTER 5

1) 1968

Griselda's nails felt just the right amount of sharp, Alberto found himself thinking, as she rolled her hips atop of him, and dug her nails into his chest. He liked the pain. He liked her. The moment Alberto Bravo meant Griselda; he knew she was special; he knew he would have her. Her hand slipped to his throat, her fingers clenched tight, and her speed picked up. A pulsing tightening deep through the very core of his being gripped his body as he held back his bliss for as long as he could. His eyes rolling in the back of his head like he was going to die. And hell, if he did, it would've been well worth it. Griselda moaned loudly, bursting out in grunting thrusts of gleeful pleasure, as her entire body moved like a wave a top of Alberto. Then her body went rigid, stiff, jerking, and her head shot back, as everything shook like she was being electrocuted. Her body gripped his like it was trying to squeeze everything from it. Alberto joined her, in the gasping erupting pleasure, as her nails dug so tightly into his neck, he'd eventually notice he was bleeding.

Alberto laid beside Griselda, his heart racing, as he dragged on a cigarette and wiped the blood from his neck with a hand towel. Griselda's breasts heaved. Sweat percolated on her chest, and her skin glistened.

"This has definitely been one of my better arrangements," Alberto said.

Griselda huffed a laugh and sat up in bed. "I think it's been profitable for the both of us."

"Your husband really thinks it takes two days to pick up fifty pounds of weed?" he laughed.

"He's out of state, running some people into America."

"If he has so many ins to America, you know you could move a lot more in America, for a lot more money."

"Carlos doesn't have that..." She looked away and thought about what to say. Griselda was long now disillusioned with Zulma 'Carlos' Trujillo. Whenever he came home, he smelled of pussy and alcohol more than anything else, and he sat in pride of the weed business he had nothing to do with. "He doesn't have that ambition. He's not like you..." Griselda reached her hand beneath the sheets and grabbed his manhood tightly in her grip. He moaned pleasantly, shifting his hips, and offering the cigarette between his fingers for her to suck on, while he pleasantly took her nipple into his mouth. "You see things. You see opportunities. New roads. You're always UP for the challenge."

"You took Carlos's operation, that was moving a measly few pounds, and turned it into one of my biggest areas of operation. I have to move more weed over the mountains to keep up with you. You're no small act yourself," Carlos praised.

"Wouldn't have been possible without you trusting me to do it."

"You gave me a good reason to trust. More than just your body that night. You laid out a simple plan half the fucking people I have working, moving product right now couldn't articulate. And unlike most motherfuckers I've dealt with... You made that shit a fucking reality." Carlos stubbed the cigarette out on the side table, with little care for the hotel's furniture, and he grabbed Griselda and tossed her on her back. Alberto didn't quite understand the captivation that he felt with her. He'd been with many women, many that were more beautiful than her, more refined than her, richer than her, and most certainly had less baggage. But there was something captivating in her eyes, something that entranced him, something that scared him as much as it excited him. He shoved his body between her thighs and pressed her hands against the headboard. He never felt this way about another woman.

Griselda wasn't content with finally making money, with having tens of thousands of dollars hidden away on her property, stored away in accounts, being something she had never thought she'd be in her life... comfortable and safe. But with Alberto, that was all possible. With Alberto, that was all likely. With Alberto... His lips were hot, his hands strong, and he always had a pleasant scent to him. A haze of cologne and good living, unlike the sweaty raunch that seeped from Carlos's pores, like the man was rotting from the inside out.

"Did you talk to Carlos about those papers?" He hovered over her body, his mouth sliding down to her neck.

"I will," Griselda said. "When he comes back. I already told him I had someone looking for papers and that will pay a lot of money."

"I don't get a discount for taking care of his wife so well?" Carlos said, thrusting forward into her.

She wrapped her legs around him. She hadn't had a man with as much stamina or recovery since Rafi, and he was sixteen at the time. Carlos could get it up. Alberto kept it up. Alberto was a man. A very well-established man, whose empire was only growing every day. And he was big and pleasant and knew how to fuck. "I think you're just going to have to enjoy this…"

2)

Griselda stared at her boys as they looked beneath the Christmas tree at all the gifts that she had put under there for them. It was the twenty-third and they had been trying to figure out what she got them since she set up the tree and put the gifts under it on the 14th. It was a holiday that never meant anything to her for most of her life, and yet, now, she was so amazed that she could make it mean something for her boys. HER BOYS. They put their ears next to the boxes, shaking them, trying to guess what was in them. She couldn't wait until Christmas morning for them to open their gifts.

She wasn't a huge fan of the Christmas tree itself. It played on her allergies a bit, her eyes running, her nose stuffy. "Enough playing with your gifts underneath the tree," said Griselda. "You have to wait. Besides, El Niño Dios has even more gifts for you."

"Also, Papa Noel may just stop by if you're good." Just as she said that, there was a knock on the door. "Who could that be?"

The boys got excited and Griselda went to the door and looked through the peephole, and then opened it.

Alberto burst through the door, dressed as Papa Noel, with a big fake white beard on his brown face, a red stocking hat, and a pillow stuffed in his stomach. "Ho, Ho, Ho," he said cheerily. Her youngest, Uber and Osvaldo, got excited, jumping up and down and screaming that it was Papa Noel. "Now, you boys have been so good... I didn't have room in your shoes for the gifts I wanted to leave you." He swung a sack off his shoulder and put it on the floor. The boys smiled and laughed excitedly. Dixon was the least sold on the matter, but when Papa Noel reached in and pulled a large box to hand to Dixon first, his demeanor slowly changed. He took it cautiously, always more aware than his brothers of the situation that was unfolding in front of them.

It was two days ago, when he saw his mother kissing another man, another man that looked a lot like Papa Noel did now. He said nothing. For Dixon, his father was a monster, a drunk, and always complaining. A scar that was above his right eye was from his father beating him with a belt and catching his face with the buckle. He hoped his mother would find someone better, even if he didn't know what that meant. But he didn't know this man either. He stared at the gift. "Open it Dixon. It's a special gift from Papa Noel." He peeled back the paper reluctantly. His face went from distrusting to smiling as he saw it. A Matchbox Motorized Speedway.

"Ay dios mio!" he exclaimed as his brothers rushed over to see it.

"I got stuff for all of you. If you were good boys for your chuchita. Were you good boys for your chuchita?"

The two nodded in the boyish, innocent way that young boys nod when they hope that the things that might make them liars aren't known. Sharing conspicuous looks with one another, they brought their attention to Papa Noel.

"I don't know. Let me ask your mother," he teased them. "Have they been good boys?"

"Hmmm…" Griselda played along.

"Mama! We've been good. We'll be better. We promise!" Osvaldo and Uber both said.

"Okay, they've been good boys."

"Well, let Papa Noel see if he has something good for Uber and Osvaldo."

"You know our names?" Uber asked in astonishment.

"Of course, Papa Noel knows your name. How would Papa Noel know what gifts to give each of you? In fact, I got you all special things." He pulled one box off and handed it to Uber, who tore into it like a wild animal and screamed joyously when he saw the electronic steam roller with remote control. He handed Osvaldo two boxes that were almost completely torn open before they left his hands. His little hands playfully grabbing everything. "You'll have to use these with your brothers and don't swallow any. You have to promise, no swallowing the toys."

"Okay, Papa Noel." He stared at the Hot Wheels Race Track and a box full of hot wheels, like he was a kettle on the stove whose stop was about to burst.

"I got you all something to play as a family as well."

"You really didn't have to do so much, Papa Noel," Griselda said.

"Nonsense… Good boys deserve all the fun they can have."

"Yeah, mom…" Uber said.

He pulled another box and Uber and Osvaldo grabbed it together, while Dixon was already setting up his track in the middle of the living room floor. The house was becoming chaotic. Griselda's usual response was to try and enforce some order, but she was fighting it, as she watched the boys cheer, when they opened the last gift which had Twister. Her usual response was to tell him to set it up in their rooms. They all had their own rooms now, so they could. But she loved seeing them play.

Alberto's hand slipped down and grabbed her ass and gave it a squeeze. She smirked in his direction, slapping his hand away while her children were distracted. "Well, Papa Noel... I guess you should probably get going."

"You sure? I might have some gifts for you." He reached into his bag before she could objection and pulled out a long narrow box. "Santa couldn't forget about the momma of the house."

She opened the jewelry box and inside was a crystal diamond necklace that glittered with a gorgeous sheen, and sparkled in her eyes. "Santa you shouldn't have."

"What did Santa get you, mommy?" Uber asked, while he struggled with the batteries in the remote of his toy.

"Something special for mommy," Griselda said, appreciating the jewelry on her wrist.

"I guess I'll have to get the carrots out later to feed the donkey," he whispered.

"You're naughty... get going."

Alberto laughed in a Chrstimasy Papa Noel chuckle, wishing the kids a goodnight, and a good Christmas before leaving the apartment.

Sitting on a plush white couch, Griselda had placed all three of her sons in front of her, as they wiggled nervously in their seat. Griselda sat on the mahogany table. Her youngest fiddled with his toy, while her two oldest gave her a stressed attention, wanting to get back to playing with their toys.

Griselda knew she had to tell them. That they had to be ready to move when the time was right. They loved the comfort of their new place. She loved that her boys were comfortable. Happy. Privileged like she never was when she grew up. And she would stay, she thought, if her children wouldn't go with her, if they'd choose their father over her.

But she had such high hopes for them. She was even thinking of putting Osvaldo in school, not that he'd learn more in some building of people that never had to learn the real world than they would with her, but it would be nice. She looked at her boys. Each handsome, strong, and capable. Real Colombian Men, not like their father.

"What would you all think about leaving Colombia?" she asked Dixon and Uber.

"Forever?"

"For a time."

"Why?" Uber asked.

"Because it would be nice to see the world. See places we've never been to."

"With father?" Dixon asked with some hesitancy. She knew Dixon knew something. He was smart, like her. He saw around corners and knew how to keep his mouth shut. And he wasn't absent of what his father was doing. She knew his hatred for his father and she was counting on that animosity. Because if he was going, they all would go. They looked up to their older brother.

Besides, none of the boys liked their father very much. If anything, they looked forward to him leaving. And it was the only time when they felt actually safe.

"Let's say not with your father?"

The boys' eyes opened wider, their interest far more piqued. They sat up straighter, and Uber put his hand on Osvaldo's hot wheel to get his attention. "Where would we go?"

"I thought we could start in America... New York... like what we've seen in the movies." Griselda smiled broadly, trying to get the apprehension from her children and get them as excited as she was.

"America? But how?" Uber asked.

"You don't trust your mother? You don't think she has her ways, that she has some tricks up her sleeves and can get her boys to America?" She grinned playfully and they smiled back at her.

"But what about dad?"

"Your father and I will be getting a divorce. I haven't told him yet. But he'll understand and see it's the best route going forward for all of us. We're too big for Colombia."

"We're too big for Colombia?" Osvaldo asked.

"That's right Osvaldo. We need a country that can hold our greatness."

"But will dad really let us go?"

"I'll take care of that!"

3)

Carlos's hand cracked across Griselda's face and she felt her jaw click as she stumbled on her feet. Tears burst to her eyes as her face scrunched up with anger.

She stumbled and spit blood on the white carpet while her children watched from the door. "Go into your rooms," she yelled at them. "Shut the door!"

"You make a fool out of me!" he screamed. "It's that motherfucker, Alberto, isn't it? Isn't it!?"

"You make a fool out of yourself," Griselda grunted, standing up straight and facing Carlos.

He had grown fatter, balder, his face worn with drink and whatever other drug he could snort or pop or smoke. Meeting his hollow eyes with hers, she glared at him, her bloody teeth cinched tight. "You can be a whore wherever you want to be, but if you think you're taking my boys, you're more fucking stupid than I ever thought you were."

"They're my boys," she said. "It's a disgrace that you had anything to do with making them."

Carlos grinned and nodded his head, biting his lip and clearing the few feet between them before he drove his fist into her stomach. Her body collapsed onto the ground and her mouth gaped open as spit and dribble mixed into the blood and poured more onto the carpet. Carlos grabbed Griselda by the hair and twisted her head so she looked at him. "I'm still your fucking husband! You will treat me with fucking respect!" He drove his fist into her face and she collapsed onto the floor. "I've supplied everything for you. You have all of this because of me. And you're going to betray me like this? You're going to try to make a fool of me? You're going to try to steal my kids from me?"

He walked over to the bar and poured himself a drink, while she worked her way to her knees and crawled on the floor away from him. Griselda had expected such a reaction. She had expected him to hit her, punch her, to gloat over her... hell, she even expected him to stop and get a drink in the process. What Carlos didn't expect was the gun Griselda hid under the table that she crawled herself to and then pulled out.

Carlos turned to her, a smile still on his face, while he cupped an ice cube in his palm, and rubbed it gingerly over his knuckles. "I'm taking my boys with me," said Griselda.

"Over my dead body," he said.

"That's always been the plan, Carlos," she moaned, raising the gun and pulling the trigger.

His eyes widened when he realized it. The pain shot through his chest. His drink flew from his hand. His body shot backwards against the bar, glass shattering on the floor. She pulled the trigger again and again and again. He slumped back, his eyes blinking furiously in the dark, his face pale and blood dripping from nearly every orifice.

Griselda struggled to her feet, wiping the blood from the side of her mouth, and walking over to Carlos. She loomed over him like a God. She felt the power of one. "I've let you think you're in charge long enough. I'm the one in charge. This is my business. This is my work. And I'll be damned if you take credit for it."

Carlos looked at her, his eyes blinking furiously, trying as he might to hold on to the last bit of life, to the last bit of consciousness that kept him tethered to this world. Needing it. Wanting it. Desiring it. Knowing he couldn't have it, no matter how much he wanted it. She aimed the gun at his head and he stared down the long black barrel. The last thought in his head was that he should've left her in that damn brothel those years ago. The last thing through his head was a bullet.

"Stay in your rooms!" she yelled at her children. "Stay in your rooms!"

She heard the doors shut tight. She had a mess on her hands. But no one in this neighborhood would alert authorities. Especially not in her apartment. No. She had time. She had plenty of time.

Going over to a desk, she sat down, and she opened the drawer and got out the passports for her and her children. She stood on unsteady legs; the adrenaline pumping through her veins, and made her way to her bedroom. She stared at her bruised eye and busted lip, at the swelling in her cheek in the vanity mirror.

Griselda stood up and went to her bed and grabbed the comforter from it. She walked back outside and over to Carlos's dead body and draped the comforter over him and his blood on the floor. Then she stepped around him and grabbed a bottle that hadn't broken from the bar and opened it. She took a swig of the aguardiente and turned around, keeping the bottle in her hands. Grabbing a pair of sunglasses off the table, she slid them on and walked over to Dixon's room.

Opening the door, she looked in at her three boys together, concerned, huddled in the corner. Their eyes were wide with horror at their mother's face, her fat lip, bloody nose, swollen eye. "Pack a bag for you and your brother. We're going to go to America."

4)

Alberto grabbed her face, twisting it left and right. "I'll kill him!" Alberto said furiously. "I'll chop his cock off and feed it to the motherfucker." His voice was a whisper, trying to keep from being too loud and scaring the boys. He gently cupped her face in his palm, running his fingers over the bruise as she winced beneath him.

Griselda and Alberto were in the bathroom together, while her children were on the hotel bed, sitting and waiting for them. She reached into her purse and pulled out the passports for her and her children and the one she had forged for him a while back. She was waiting, waiting for something like this, waiting for the moment that she could be done with Carlos, and run off with Alberto. "He's dead. His body is in the apartment."

"You killed him?"

"I didn't have a choice," Griselda said, hugging Alberto and sniffling on his shoulder.

Alberto gripped her tight and held her in his grasp. He kissed the side of her cheek, the nape of her shoulder. "Don't worry. I'll take care of it. If no one called the police, I'll have my men clear the room. If anyone did, no one will find you or the kids. Don't worry about it. You understand me?" Alberto pulled away from Griselda and held her by the shoulders. "You and the boys are safe. I won't let anything happen to you."

"He had made the passport for you before he found out about us. He made a call when he got home and he went into a fury and started beating me and screaming that I had made a fool of him. But we have the passports. We can go."

"And we will! We will. We just got to get things in place here. Get the business ready to ship. But we'll go to America."

Griselda nodded, smiling on the inside, while offering as much of a sympathetic look as she could. Alberto loved her. He truly loved her. And if she was honest, she was quite fond of him. But America… that was the dream… that was the goal… that was what she wanted more than anything in the world. And now it was within reach. She hugged Alberto again and wept her fake tears onto his shoulder for another minute. "Thank you. Thank you! I don't know how I would've ever done any of this without you. I'd be poor and probably dead right now without you."

"It's okay. It's okay. I'm going to take care of everything."

"I know you will," said Griselda. "I know you will."

PART 4
MADE IN AMERICA
ALBERTO BRAVO

CHAPTER 6

1) 1970

Roberto Colomb hated these cloak and dagger meetings. A friend of his, a good friend, took a bullet during one. It was late, nearly midnight, and he was sitting in an abandoned lot, smoking his third cigarette for the night to keep his nerves calm, even though he promised his wife he was going to quit two weeks ago. "This motherfucker better show up," he muttered to himself.

He wasn't really inconspicuous. From the black Lincoln to his black suit and blue tie, Roberto Colomb screamed FED in a way a ten-year-old could tell the moment he stepped on any street. He liked it. The power. The respect. But not this. Not shady meetings in the dark tens of miles out of New York City, waiting on a guy who's only meeting with him to betray more powerful men. If he's willing to betray his friends, no doubt, he'd be willing to betray Roberto. His eyes were glued to his mirrors. He knew he had back-up, some people ready to help him if things went bad. But would they get there quick enough? He doubted it. He wanted to give the appearance that he trusted the son-of-a-bitch. As much as you can trust a snitch.

Car lights came off in the distance, filling the rearview mirror, and he unfastened his holster and rested his hand on his gun. A moment later, a car turned into the parking lot and pulled up beside him. Frederico Maslany got out of the vehicle. He was a tall man, with jet black hair and a hooked nose. He walked around the car and over to the passenger side, and opened the door.

Getting in, Freddy, as his friends and family knew him, sat down in a huff. "Can I bum one of those?" he asked, nodding to the cigarette tucked tightly in Roberto's lips.

Roberto reached into the inner pocket of his suit jacket and pulled out a tin cigarette holder case and popped it open with his free hand, and offered a cigarette for him. Freddy took it, slipping the cigarette between his lips. "Need a light?" Roberto asked, putting the cigarettes back and reaching into his pant pocket and pulling a lighter out for him.

Freddy drew on the cigarette for a full minute, closing his eyes and savoring the flavor. He leaned back and relaxed into the seat, taking one deep breath full of smoke after another. Grabbing the handle and rolling the window down. Frankly, Roberto was relieved. It meant he could explain away the accompanying smell of smoke with his C.I smoking in the car. She'd be skeptical. But she'd go along with it. He just needed to remember to use the mouthwash or grab something to eat at the gas station.

"What do you got for me?"

"Man, I got something big, real big!"

"Then talk… I didn't come out all this way this late at night for your shiny personality."

"You got your own task force, thanks to my information. I feel like a little thank-you is in order."

"I kept you out of prison. I feel like you giving me the information I want is probably in your best interest."

"I can't believe the government really is all tied up on catching pot dealers and shit."

"Tides are changing. Nixon doesn't like all these fucking hippies and Blacks protesting the fuck out of him. You know what hippies and Blacks have in common?"

"I don't know, a liking for sexually liberated white women? A want for equal rights?"

"Drugs… they all do fucking drugs."

"I'm just fucking with you. I don't got any love loss for jigaboos or hippies. My old man fought in World War 2 and I would've fought in Nam, but got flat feet, you know. Kept me out of the fucking war." He lifted a foot and started playing with the leather sole of his shoe.

"I really don't give a fuck about your feet," Roberto said.

"That's hurtful," laughed Freddy, sliding his foot back down. "Here I am thinking we're friends."

"We're not. You're an informant. I keep you out of prison for the laundry list of crimes I have you dead to rights to. And you give me information. You're not living up to your half and that's really starting to piss me off. I want to get home to my wife. So talk."

"Some Colombians have moved into New York. Initially, for the first six months, they were keeping to themselves. Just fueling the spic and nigger market. Moving a lot, but staying out of white areas. But now they're making deals with the Bonanno's and trying to get in other Family business, get their drugs distributed across the country. They're moving a lot of weed. I mean, they're moving a lot of weed. And not the shit you're all used to, either. No... Good shit. And people are eating it up."

"They're working with the Bonanno's?"

"Yeah, the Bonanno's, the Richi... several people are buying up their weed."

"So the Bonanno's are getting heavy into the weed market? That's what you're telling me?"

"Weed, a little cocaine, some speed..."

"And who are the Colombians?"

"I'm keeping my ear to the ground. Right now, everyone I know just calls them The Colombians. They're on the move constantly. They keep a low profile. They're pretty much fucking ghosts right now. At least to most of us. It's a man and a woman running it. I think they're husband and wife. The woman they say is loco. What I heard was that one of her distributors was rude to her, called her a bitch, and she cut out his fucking tongue while he was alive, before putting a bullet in him. I don't know if it's true. These Colombians, man, they don't screw around out here."

Roberto was interested. More on the Bonanno's than any foreign dealers. Drugs might have been a priority for the government in rhetoric, but the FBI was about getting someone that would make headlines. Two Colombians bringing weed in the country meant nothing. You didn't make your name on a big bust of drugs... but you did make your name on taking down a crime family like the Bonanno's. "I'm going to need more than some fucking Colombians. And I want to know the Bonanno's operation."

"That's a lot to fucking ask."

"We let you run that illegal casino without cops interfering, so you can be a hub for these people. You're making out well. Unless you don't want to make out well," Roberto said.

Freddy smiled and nodded as he finished up the cigarette. "I'll get working on it."

"Work harder!"

"I'll get you more, but come on, you didn't know that there were fucking Colombians running around moving pallets of weed. You've got information. Aren't you supposed to do policing and stuff?"

"What do you think I'm doing? I can always start cracking down on bookmaking, illegal gambling, and the litany of shit that I have on you... not to mention your wife and your mistress... and your girlfriend..."

"You're mean," said Freddy. "That's just mean. You gonna bring my girlfriend into this? Kathy hasn't done anything wrong. We're supposed to have a relationship built on respect. I'm not feeling very respected."

"Our relationship is you give me information and you stay out of prison. ACTIONABLE INFORMATION. Not mystery Colombians. But give me some information on the Bonanno's operation. Give some information that I can actually use. Anything else you're expecting from this, you better go down to the fucking bath houses."

"You're a real... asshole. I'll get you more information. Right now, that's what I got. Colombians are making big moves in the pot market, and cocaine is starting to show up in my casino. Did I tell you that? A few guys are doing it."

"Is there a market for that?" Roberto asked. Cocaine had largely disappeared from the government's purview by the 1950s. There were a couple of Beatniks and the such that were trying to make something of it in the 1960s, but by and large, the DEA wasn't looking at cocaine. But it was something for Roberto to note. Something for him to consider, but not what he was looking for when he was thinking the man was going to give him information.

"It's a growing market."

"What type of growing market?"

"I don't know. I just know that a good amount of people in my establishment are partaking in the white powder. What do you want from me…" Freddy tossed his hands up, exasperated, not expecting all his information to be so easily dismissed.

"More!" Roberto said. "I want more!"

Freddy shook his head. "Look, they're focused on the Colombian pot. If you talk to cops, that's what they're all going to be talking about, right, like an immense wave of high-end weed. I mean potent shit. You're talking three to four puffs and you're on your ass staring at the ceiling. It's good shit and they're bringing in a lot of it. How is that not information?"

"Get me some names. Get me some locations. Get me something that I can put people on and I'll agree that it's something."

"You just always want stuff," said Freddy. "Can I get another smoke?"

"Get out of my car Freddy."

"Really? It's gonna be like that?"

"Out of the car Freddy, and get me the information I want. Don't have me drag my ass back out her for some shit like this. Okay? You bring me out to an abandoned lot all by myself, you better be trying to kill me, or bringing me something that's actually useable."

Freddy pursed his lips. "Alone?" he laughed. "Please, you feds think you're clever... You don't think I didn't spot the two cars parked up the block, or the fucking homeless guy that's out here in the middle of nowhere, with no bar or liquor store for three miles, sleeping on a fucking bench? No... don't think you're clever. But don't worry... I don't hold it against you... I wouldn't trust me either."

"Just bring me names and places... or next time these conversations could end a lot different," Roberto said, not trying to show any amusement or sign of being impressed. Freddy didn't strike him as the observant type at all.

Freddy patted him on the shoulder. "Alright, I heard you the first ten times. Nice talk! I'll be in touch!"

"I'll be in touch..."

"Whatever you want, Roberto."

"Agent Colomb of the FBI, don't forget it!"

"Agent Colomb then," Freddy said mockingly, getting out of the car. "The might and powerful Agent Roberto Colomb..."

Roberto watched him and waited. Once Freddy left, Roberto pulled out his radio. "Do we have any information on some Colombians doing business in the weed market?"

CHAPTER 7

1) 1970

Griselda looked out the window of the airplane as the cityscape of New York came into view. The statue of liberty stood majestically in the mix of everything, gorgeous and amazing, greeting them to their new land. Her boys behind her battled over the view, little Osvaldo struggling to get his little head into the window, until they were told to fasten their seatbelts. Alberto was excited. It wasn't their first trip to America. They'd gone several times to make sure that everything was set up, that the dealers were in place, that the routes for shipping the drugs were solid. More importantly, coming in and out of New York gave them an elusiveness that made it impossible for anyone to pin them down. They invested in safe houses, on Griselda's suggestion, while they worked out of hotels. Any contact with a potential buyer was met with protocols to make sure no one followed them, or tracked them, and no one could figure out who they were, or where they were operating from.

Alberto was amazed, even though he knew he shouldn't be, at how quickly Griselda picked up this life.

For all intents and purposes, no one thought they lived in the country, and that was how Griselda liked it. Because now, this flight, after six months, was to make their life in New York official. Alberto squeezed her hand and grinned at her.

She made it, she thought. Killing, stealing, whoring, trafficking... she had made it to the land of opportunity. She had actually made it. She was going to be an American. Raise her children in the land of opportunity and freedom. The place of movies. The place where she could truly become who she was always meant to be.

The apartment they rented looked out over New York City. Griselda had grown accustom to the view in all the hotels they stayed at. It was important to her they have a place that had a magnificent view. Even if it meant eating into a lot more money than they initially thought. None of that mattered. None of it. She and Alberto were already making plenty of money and with everything set up and in place, they were going to be making a lot more now that everything was going. Wealth and riches were the only thing on her mind.

She loved the city. The moment she stepped foot in it, she loved it. It was so much different from Colombia. It's brilliant city lights sparkling like a sea of stars in the nighttime. The streets had their own music, their own life to them, their own majesty... a gorgeous aliveness that she felt might beat Colombia. This was its own kind of jungle, a cement jungle, a wild living animal that would eat alive anyone not ready for it. But she was ready. She was ready to tame the beast.

Their apartment was bigger than what they had in Colombia and what they had in Colombia was pretty big. Albert wondered if they could be drawing an eye to themselves, but Griselda seemed dead set on the apartment in the middle of New York City. A limestone fireplace sat in the living room, with the biggest television the kids had ever seen beside it. It took three men to hall the behemoth up into the elevator and into the apartment. They even had to take the door off to get it into their home. But it was worth it. The kids screamed excitedly and in sheer awe. Not to mention, it had color, and they hadn't had a color TV before.

The kids were in heaven. Griselda was happy. Alberto was comfortable. And both of them were ready to get to work.

Griselda went with him to see the operation when they first arrived. Though she didn't plan on putting her face out there much, since if things did go wrong, someone needed to stay out of prison to keep things going. When they first came here, the connections Albert had had a pretty decent network of dealers and processing houses, but it wasn't nearly ready for the business that they were going to bring in. It took them four months in Colombia before they could leave, brokering new deals with growers, buying up land, and setting things in place with their people in Colombia, to keep that operation running, so if they had to return, they didn't have to rebuild.

When they first arrived, they had three distributors; two were Black, and only one was Colombian, which bothered Griselda. Not that the men were Black. She couldn't care one bit about the race of anyone. She just liked people that spoke her language, since she hadn't yet gotten great at speaking English. But she quickly got over it. The two Black men, Raymond and Marcus, were actually far more put together, safe and respectful than Julio. "You can't be running an operation like ours and acting a fool out on the street. Cops see niggers acting out and getting rowdy and the next thing you know, your home is raided and cops put two in the back of your head."

Julio didn't have such reservations. He wore a garish watch, spoke in big and prideful ways about how smart he was, and had little security or plans in case things went wrong. That Alberto even trusted this man with anything to begin with made her question his sanity. But what sealed it for her, what got his name written on her must-kill list, was that he twice ignored her questions and treated her like a nuisance... Then he said, "Why'd you bring the bitch? Am I not doing business with you?"

"I'll wait outside, Alberto," she said.

She wanted to kill him, but she knew that would send the wrong message so early in their development... they needed more distributors first... then she'd kill him.

Within three months, they took over most of the Bronx and Queens and expanded their distribution network to six other people. Really five, and one to replace Julio. Because if there was one thing Griselda didn't do, it was forget when she was slighted. And now, with the operations growing, and her suspicions about Julio's operation being subpar, a robbery in their first few months of business, something neither Marcus nor Raymond had to deal with? She had gotten the GreenLight to take care of him as she chose.

Griselda wanted to make a show of it. Shooting a guy in the face was something that would make other people think twice about crossing her or Alberto. But she had a plan, a proper plan, one that would make noise in all the right places. Even if it involved putting a lot of her own money up to get it done.

"You don't have enough security," she said. "We thought we'd help you with that." She had a group of five men, toughs, who knew they were going to get dirty today, come in behind her.

"I don't need your help. I just need the pot. Fucking women don't seem to get how business works."

"We should go to your office and talk," said Griselda.

"Porque?"

"Because I want to talk to you," said Griselda.

Julio rolled his eyes. "Listen bitch. I'm making you a lot of money. When I last came from Colombia, women seem to know their place. I don't know if all this American Feminism bullshit is getting into your head. But I don't take advice from putas. I don't care who your husband is. I've been selling drugs here for five years. You've just come here."

"You know, you're very disrespectful," said Griselda. "You ought to watch your tongue around me."

"And you ought to know who the fuck you're messing with." They were in an apartment, one that he had turned into a pseudo-office, and he had several men sitting around, as his own security of sorts. He showed them off with a wave of his hand like that was to intimidate her. "I've got my own men."

"And you should know who's paying them," said Griselda. Julio tilted his head. "Leave!" she ordered.

In a minute, the men that had worked with Julio for years, his friend that had been there with him since he started it, got up and left, looking at him woefully and apologetically. "What the fuck is this?"

"I rarely find men to be loyal too much. Money, power, threats to their families and their loved ones, and they'll largely do whatever you want them to. I didn't even have to threaten anyone. Your mistake was thinking that I'm some puta here playing checkers, trying to get everything in place," Griselda snarled. "This isn't checkers. This is chess, and I'm the queen. I'm the most powerful fucking piece there is."

Julio went to reach for the gun he kept in the back of his pants, but the men Griselda brought tackled him to the ground, before he could even get it untucked from his trousers. "Fucking betrayal!" he yelled. "Betrayal!"

"Yes, yes, get out everything you have to say," said Griselda. The men seized his arms behind him as he continued to struggle and took the gun from him.

He fought. He fought as hard as he could. It just wasn't enough against the men she brought. They bound his arms behind him on the frame of the chair with duct tape and then his legs to the legs of the chair. When he was fully immobile, one man pulled open Julio's mouth and another grabbed his tongue with a pair of pliers, turning his head away, not wanting to see what Griselda was going to do. "You disrespected me for the last fucking time," said Griselda, as she took out a knife from her purse.

Julio screamed so loud Griselda's ears would ring all day. Each octave, coming out louder and louder, as she severed his tongue from his mouth. His head collapsed forward when they let go of him and blood poured from his mouth into a puddle on his lap. "Are we going to leave him like this?"

Griselda stared at him. It would serve him right. But she knew she'd be looking over her shoulder if she did. "Gun," she said, and one man handed her a gun.

"Don't say I'm not merciful," she laughed, and then pulled the trigger.

The rumors were plenty. From skinning him alive, to cutting off his penis. Whenever Griselda walked into a room with Alberto after that, the men were immediately respectful of her.

More than that, they were already moving a hundred pounds a month and were looking to expand the business outward even more and get it up to three hundred or four hundred pounds of pot before the end of the year.

Six months in, they were distributing to Pennsylvania, the Bronx, and Queens. The Irish had most of Brooklyn and Massachusetts and the Italians with the Jews controlled Manhattan and Connecticut.

For a while, all of that was acceptable. Before they were living there, that was acceptable. But Griselda didn't move to another country to live an acceptable life. Though Alberto was content with growing the business slowly, being a top-end distributor to his small gaggle of undesirables, who the closest they came to white America was selling weed in Washington Park or to the working class in Pennsylvania, Griselda knew that regardless of where they were, what was true in Colombia was true in America, doubly so. You grow or you die. She wanted the respect that their weed should bring. That they *deserved*.

The respect that bringing top end product into the country ought to have.

With her children entertaining themselves in front of the television. She had taught Dixon how to use the phone and call 911 if something bad happened (not 123, as it was in Colombia). She felt safe in letting them stay alone. She was alone plenty at their age. Alberto was off, dealing with the business, and being the face of the business. With shipments that were about to come in, he was making sure the proper hands were greased and that everything came in without a hitch.

Griselda dawned wigs, changed clothes, and disappeared into New York in only the way one can disappear in New York. It took her some time, going into a few bars and playing the flirty Latin women, looking for a little attention and fun. But she found dealers in Manhattan and Brooklyn and bought dime bags up and down the neighborhoods until she felt she had a good enough sample.

Back home, she sent the boys into their room, and she rolled joints from each and every one of the dime bags, put on a Curtis Mayfield album, and started testing the weed. She knew the moment she sucked on the joint and a seed popped that people were getting shit for weed. Most of the weed was seeds and sticks. Poorly grown at that, not separating male and female. Their growers back in Colombia knew what they were doing and maybe it was the Colombian soil, or the natural rain, but their stuff was massively more potent.

"You smoking without me?" Alberto asked, coming into the apartment and taking off his shoes at the door. It was May, but far chillier than he was ever used to in Colombia, and he still was wearing his winter coat, even though it was a nice sixty degrees.

"You know what this is, Alberto?"

"Cannabis?"

"Competition. Shitty fucking competition, but competition."

"What'd you do?"

"I went shopping."

"What do you mean, you went shopping?" He walked over to the couch and looked at the baggies of weed laid out on the table.

"I checked out what people are selling as weed, so I knew how it compared to our product. These poor people, they don't even know what good stuff is if they're buying this trash. I've been smoking for a little while and I'm barely fucking buzzed." She stubbed a joint out on the table. "We need to meet the Italians and the Irish and get them selling our stuff."

"Or get them to put a bullet in our heads."

Griselda laughed with her whole body heaving forward. "They're business people. We're stupid Colombians to them. We underbid the market, take a smaller profit, get in their network, then when everyone loves what they're getting, we raise the prices claiming import costs. It's simple."

"You're devious."

"Ambitious."

"Ambitious," Alberto corrected, sitting down beside her and turning and kissing her. "Where are the kids?"

"In their room."

"Boys!" he yelled. "Get out here!"

Osvaldo, Uber, and Dixon came out of the room. "Here's five bucks, don't get arrested, go do something fun... don't come back for an hour!"

"Things are more expensive here," Dixon said.

Alberto glinted at him. Happy a little that Dixon had stopped being passive to him, a little annoyed that he was being shaken down by a near ten-year-old."

"Your boys are just as good as you at business."

135

"They ought to be," said Griselda, nodding approvingly at her son, who smiled and gathered his brothers underneath his arms. The sun was still up. There were plenty of things for them to do. An Ice Cream shop down the street. A pinball machine at a pizza shop. And a park across the street that they hung out at all the time.

When the door shut, Alberto brought his attention back to Griselda, his hand snaking beneath her shirt as he kissed her neck. "You're either going to get us killed, or you're going to make us rich," he told her.

2)

"Why do we need to do business with a bunch of spics that barely speak the language?" Michael Binoche asked. He was their first contact with the Bonanno crime family.

"Because in the six months we've been here, we've moved nearly two thousand pounds of weed while staying out of your neighborhoods. People from Brooklyn and Manhattan are coming to our communities to get weed. Our weed is top-notch, high end, and potent," said Alberto. Griselda sat quietly, taking in Michael Binoche. His Italian suit, his greased back hair. He was a living stereotype of a 1940s gangster, right down to the drawled New York accent.

They were in a club in Downtown Manhattan, a Sinatra look-alike was singing Fly Me To The Moon on stage, while women in skimpy black outfits wandered around the smoke-filled rooms, with trays of drink and cigarettes, all while dodging playful hands.

"How much better?" Michael asked.

Griselda pulled out a joint from her bag and lit it, puffing it in, leaving a little red from her lipstick around the paper, before handing it to him.

The man looked at it and smelled it. "Don't smell any different."

"Just smoke it," she said.

He brought it tentatively to his lips and sucked it in a big gulping drag. His face paled slightly as he coughed and gagged and heaved clouds of smoke from his lungs. "Figure, white boys can't hold their weed," said Griselda to Alberto in Spanish.

"Be nice," he replied.

"Speak English," Michael coughed again, his face blood red, as he finally got his breath back. He looked at the joint, admiring it now. He cleared his throat and took a much smaller hit and sucked it in and held it. "Alright... Alright..." He exhaled a smaller cloud of smoke. "You got my attention."

"Of course, we do," said Griselda.

3) 1971

"I love the fucking Cheetah Club," said Griselda, as she sat down, sweating, slipping her heels off her sore feet and tossing them into Alberto's lap. He grabbed her feet and massaged them for her, while Fania All Stars played "Bamboleo" on stage, and girls danced in matching scantily-clad leopard prints. The music was great. The band perfect. And though she hated to admit it, Alberto was right, she needed this. Children, drug dealers, and dealing with dirty cops and freight inspectors to make sure their shipments were coming in undisturbed was definitely draining. Staying ahead of the mob, making sure that they weren't fucking with the books, or trying to fuck their money, was another problem. It required a lot of energy and stress, and for the last month or two, as they've been trying to get as much product into the hands of everyone involved, she had been exhausted.

The music surged through her body and danced in her soul. Fania All Stars was one of her favorite bands and it felt good to be surrounded by her own people, to be able to speak Spanish without people staring at her, or those fucking Italians telling her to speak English even as they throw around their poor Italian. The people were amazing too. The alcohol delicious. But for the first time in a long time, she was feeling her age.

Alberto was sweating a bit more than usual. His leg was jittering up and down, shaking her thigh. "You ready to dance again?" he asked. Something seemed off in him. She had thought so, but now she was positive.

Griselda stared at him questioningly, trying to figure out what was going on with him. He was always passionate, a Latin man through and through, seductive and fun. But he seemed to be much more energized than usual, dancing all about, moving with abandon. Sporting a semi-erection whenever he was rubbing up against her.

"What's gotten into you?"

Albert laughed. "Nothing... the night, you..."

"And?"

"Guys were doing coke in el baño..."

"Cocaine?"

"Si."

"Our coke?"

"No."

"Was it good?"

"Not as good as what we got. Some Peruvian shit, I'm guessing."

"You didn't bring me any?"

"Wasn't mine," said Alberto, his hand digging into the center of her foot, causing her to pleasantly sigh.

"Well, I'm going to the bathroom and then we can dance," Griselda said, taking her feet back and sliding on her heels.

"Hurry back," Alberto urged, pinching her ass as she walked by him.

The Cheetah club had largely become their place to hang out, and word was that it was closing soon, so they were trying to get as much time in it as they could. They always had a good night when they came home. The kids passed out. The apartment theirs. It was always an excellent opportunity to unwind from an otherwise stressful life. In the dark of the club, there was an intimacy even as the floor was packed with people. Something about lying against Alberto's chest, feeling his fingers run up her hips, feeling his heart against her back, as she slipped her way down his body, made her feel so peaceful.

They always had a table, because the owner was one of the few people that bought the small amount of cocaine that they shipped in for the local market. They were requiring a little more than usual over the last few months, but Griselda wasn't thinking much about it.

In the bathroom, women were gathered around each other in the corner of the sink and as one woman would lean forward, other women would hold her hair for her, and that familiar snorting rip caught Griselda's interest. She had largely put her cocaine use behind her, because they didn't have basuco in New York. She was fond of cocaine, but they weren't transporting enough for her to feel like it was worth diving into. This was new, though. Groups of people enjoying lines of coke. "Having fun?" she asked, as a girl stood up and wiped her nose, her eyes wide and pleasant.

"Very much so. You want some?"

Griselda did her lipstick in the mirror, ignoring them for a second, and then looked at them. She shrugged and said, "Sure, I'll do a line."

It was plain, cut poorly, and a bit uneventful. "How much did you pay for this?"

"Twenty a gram," she said casually. "A little less cause my guy bought in bulk. It's good stuff, right?"

She rubbed her nose of the burn and wiped her eyes. "Your shits' cut horribly. It's not worth five dollars, let alone twenty," said Griselda, turning away from the women as they gawked at her offendedly. Twenty a gram. Twenty a gram. They were moving a couple pounds to distributors at less than four a gram. And their stuff was pure. It made the shit she just snorted look like baking powder, which she was pretty certain was eighty percent of what she snorted.

Moving through the dance floor, she tossed herself onto Alberto's lap. "Do you know how much they're paying for coke?"

"Eight or ten a gram?"

"Twenty... twenty a fucking a gram."

"No shit!" Alberto said.

"No fucking shit, and they were snorting a bunch. I think there might be a bigger market for coke out here," she said excitedly as the band started playing "Ella Agua De Bellen." The coke was kicking in and she was feeling it now and ready to dance. She pushed herself off of him with a little help from Alberto.

Grabbing his hand, she pulled him onto the dance floor, yelling excitedly, "Let's dance."

4)

"Cocaine's not a big drug. No one's doing it," said Don Franco Giovanni, the head of the Rossi family, and their second largest buyer for their weed. The Bonanno family had turned them down before they even really got to say anything. The head of the family wouldn't even sit with them. But Don Giovanni believed in respect, especially for anyone that put a million dollars in his pocket.

Griselda liked him as much as she hated him. He was outwardly racist in that way that made it almost parody. He was a man who you knew where you stood with him. And that was good enough for her.

"People are starting to," said Griselda to the Don. "I've been going to the clubs. A lot of people are doing coke. It's a… um… what do you Americans say…? Up-and-coming market."

Don Franco Giovanni was the head of the Rossi family. A middle-aged man. His hair, prematurely gray from years of stressful living was combed back and flat against his head. He had a roundish face, slightly overweight, and a liking for white suits. He had a simple rather straight forward look that left little to the imagination about what type of business he was in. He was right out of the movies with his gangster styling and flailing gestures, surrounded by two heavies in sweat suits, and two other men with tight black suits, that had their hands tucked in their suit jackets, ready to draw. "Spic clubs, though, right?"

Griselda forced a tight lip smile. This was what she meant. "I don't hang out at a lot of wop clubs, don't

141

really think Frank Sinatra's all that good," Griselda shot back and Alberto stared at her, fastening his hand to his gun, in case this got ugly.

"You're a vulgar woman," the Don laughed, the gold of his fillings clear as he tossed his head back. "Don't go about insulting Frankie, though. That won't be tolerated here." He adjusted his tie. "In my younger days, I would've been interested in a little Latin seasoning like you."

"In my younger days, I would've robbed you, and had a guy ready to beat you and leave you for dead outside a club in Colombia."

"Hmm…"

"I would've been too much for you."

He snorted. "Possibly. But I doubt it. Anyway… we're not interested. You're making plenty of money with the weed. We're making plenty of money with the weed. We don't have any interest in any fucking cocaine. There's no market for it, and I don't want to get stuck with a bunch of shit. I can't move."

"That's fine, Don Giovanni," said Alberto, grabbing hold of Griselda's hand and pressing it into the wooden arm of the chair. "That's completely understandable. Thank you for your time…"

Don Giovanni nodded and signaled for them to leave.

"You wouldn't mind if we sold it on your territory, would you? If it's a product that you're not interested in, then there shouldn't be a conflict. We're not screwing you out of any territory and we're not competing with you, right?"

Don Giovanni thought about it for a moment. "You think you can sell it? Sell it wherever you like. Just as long as none of your dealers are competing with our pot, go right ahead."

"We thank you for your time," said Alberto. "We thought we'd offer you the opportunity, as a branch, for being in business with you over the last year. But we completely understand if it's not for you."

"I've been in this business a long time," said the Don. "Many a people fuck up a good business, trying to go for something else. You're making plenty of money. Living good lives. Why rock the boat with stuff you don't know?"

"Wise words," said Alberto, and Griselda shot him a hateful stare. She didn't think the words were wise at all. Were all the men in this business cowards? Did anyone of them have the cajones to actually make something grand?

Griselda slid her hand from beneath Alberto's, a frustrated flare of her nostrils, as she forced a smile. "Sorry to waste your time," she said. Griselda stood up and turned away from them and walked for the door of the Don's office.

Driving down the road, Griselda sat with her arms crossed, and her eyes staring out the window. Alberto could feel the tension. "What? We got what we wanted."

"If I say, you'll just be angry."

"Just fucking talk. What the fuck's the problem?"

"Nothing, I'm just surprised you didn't lick his ass clean after you were done kissing it all so much, acting like a fucking coño," said Griselda.

Alberto's jaw tensed, his head twisted, and suddenly, he jerked the car to the sidewalk and brought it to a sudden halt. "Who the fuck you think you're fucking talking to like that?" He grabbed her arm and dug his fingers into her tender flesh as he twisted her body in his direction. "You can play the crazy bitch role with all those motherfuckers out there. Disrespect anyone you fucking want. And I'll have your fucking back. I respect everything you've ever fucking done, Griselda. I've backed you and I'm backing you now. But you ever fucking talk to me like that again, and I'll break your fucking jaw."

Griselda smiled at him. "Calm down," she cooed, not even a bit of worry in her voice. She slipped his hand from her arm. "I'm just saying... Where was this man in the meeting?"

"Keeping us from getting shot. You're insulting Frank Sinatra. That's like insulting Jesus Christ, for God's sakes, to these men. They don't want to do business, that's fine. We didn't go there to do business. We went there, by your suggestion, to make sure they green-lit us moving dealers into their territory. Why are you pissed?"

"I'm not... I just think you could've been a little less... less...."

"You're a real perra sometimes, you know that? We've got their permission. Our dealers won't be fucked with. We'll find other avenues and distributors and afterwards they'll come crawling back to us. But your fucking mouth could get us all in trouble. Talking shit about Frank Sinatra. You fucking love Frank Sinatra!"

"I do," Griselda laughed. "I wanted to keep them off guard. It hurt me to say it." She liked it when he got aggressive with her. "I'm just saying that these motherfuckers don't know how to do crime, though."

"What?"

"Why do we even have to play these games? We could get men from Colombia up here. Some hit men. And we could kill these motherfuckers and just take over."

Alberto shook his head. Calm returning to him. Now no longer certain that his wife was being serious. "You're insane, you know that?"

"Maybe. But I'm right."

"The Five families have been trying to off each other for a decade with little success. The FBI has been coming after the mob for fifty years with little success. We are not going to be the people to kill them or take them down... but we can be the ones to eventually make a fortune from them."

"At one point, we'll become disposable. They'll look for a more direct deal, and then what... what, Alberto? They'll kill us. That's what the fuck will happen and you're just going to sit there and open your mouth and take the gun in it and let them blow your fucking brains all over the fucking floor. That's what you're going to do."

"They didn't want to do the business. This is a new enterprise. There's no reason to believe that we're going to get killed yet. We're still going to sell the coke. I'm already talking to Jose about getting up a fifty pounds of it. If we're wrong, we're going to be in trouble on that end."

"We're not wrong. We just need distributors in the more wealthy areas. We need some distributors for the white folks. Cause I'm telling you, I'm telling you... once they start using cocaine, they're going to want it endlessly. It's going to be game over. The energy, the excitement, that's just what a fucking capitalist society needs."

"We'll figure it out!"

"I'm sorry about what I said," Griselda said. "I hate being told no and hate seeing you have to humble yourself to these little bitches, when we should be the ones they're coming to. We're the ones with the fucking product. We're the ones that are responsible for making them millions. And here we are, being treated like the fucking hired help."

"Don't worry about it. Our time will come."

"When it does. We're cutting those motherfuckers out of it. And they'll fucking remember that they had the fucking chance to be at the bottom floor of this fucking opportunity and they didn't take it. That's what's going to happen. We aren't going to bring the Italians in on this at a discount, or anything. They'll pay premium prices. Fuck the Irish. You hear me? This is ours. They aren't looking at the fucking market. They are ignoring us. Refusing to meet with us. Treating us like we're fucking amateurs. They're missing a golden opportunity and we're not going to let them be our Middle Men for it for cheap," said Griselda, as she sat back in the seat and tossed her head back frustratedly.

Alberto put the car back in drive and looked in his mirror. "Whatever you say, Griselda, whatever you say! We have the territory to move it in. Let's see how it does."

CHAPTER 8

1) 1972

Griselda stepped from the plane and smelled the Colombian air with a smile. The heat danced across her face and warmed her entire body. It was winter back in New York. Snow and ice covered the streets. Here, she could already smell the Spanish cooking in the air, just lingering throughout the country. The red dirt was a welcoming sight. She didn't realize just how much she missed it, being surrounded by pavement and cement everywhere she went in New York.

She hated the winters in New York. She tried. She really tried to like them. But she just couldn't bring herself to enjoy them. The cold bit right through her. Her body never seemed to adjust to it. She had to have the heat up to the seventies and the fireplace stocked. She really didn't like the cold.

Her sons, however, didn't share hatred of the cold, nor her enthusiasm for Colombia. Looking at her boys frowning away, Griselda could only smile and shake her head. "We're back in our homeland. Be happy."

"Why are we back, though?" The boys liked the winters in New York. The two they had already. They were all getting good at speaking English with the tutors her mother bought them. And then there was the television… The television was amazing in America. Multiple channels. Tons of colored shows. Yeah, it

147

took time to get used to the cold, but once they had the sweaters and coats and gloves, they loved playing in the snow. Burying Osvaldo in it until his teeth chattered. Doing snowball fights that often ended up in real fights between Uber and Dixon when one inevitably hits the other with ice or a rock in the snowball.

But more than that, Colombia just wasn't America. They liked all the luxuries that they had back home in New York and were annoyed that they were getting dragged along back to Colombia. For Osvaldo, Colombia was barely a memory. He looked at the country like he did America when he was two, wide eyed and uncertain, full of nervousness and worry, knowing his mix of Spanish and English. But it didn't deter Griselda's enthusiasm. She couldn't be away from her kids for the months it was going to take to do what she needed to do.

"Why did we have to come?" Dixon whined.

"Because, I need my boys with me to help me set-up the business, and besides… you can't forget where you came from."

"You don't even like Colombia," Uber said.

"You don't have to like something to love it," said Griselda. "If you did, you all wouldn't be born."

"Papi Alberto didn't have to come."

"Your Papi has business to attend to. He can't be keeping an eye on your rambunctious little bums all day, every day. Besides… I need your help… we're here to open a business."

"What type of business?" Dixon asked.

"You know how mommy opened a lingerie business in America? We need to get a lingerie company up and going here that will manufacture that lingerie. We already have the warehouse. I just need to get everything in place and make sure that everything is going to be built with my specifications."

"Why?"

"Because it'll be good for business," she said with finality, in a way that said, don't ask me again, and then turned her attention to the airport lobby.

A short, dark-skinned man in an equally dark suit stood with a sign that said Bravo Familia on it. Alberto said he would get everything set up and she didn't doubt him. He had also made sure that their connections knew she was coming so that she could organize with them.

Griselda waved at the man and the man ran over, taking her carry-on bag from her hand. "Hola, Señora Bravo," said the man.

"We brought a lot of luggage, hopefully –"

"That will be no problem, Mrs. Bravo, your husband made sure of it. He paid my company well. We've got two cars ready just for you and the kids."

"Very good," said Griselda. "Then let's get going."

When Griselda first came to America, she wanted a piece of apple pie. There was nothing more American than apple pie, after all. Coming home to Colombia, the first thing Griselda wanted was some real empanadas. Outside of her own cooking, which she didn't do much of, she couldn't find good empanadas. Even when she found a good Colombian restaurant, it was made with American produce and just never tasted as good as it did in Colombia.

The driver leaned against the car, waiting for them. While her oldest children sat with their arms crossed, watching as their mother devoured one empanada after another, pushing the plate back at her when she pushed it to them, saying, "Eat, eat... they're absolutely delicious."

"We're not hungry," said Uber.

"Not hungry," Griselda said. "Not hungry... please, if I don't make my plate before I bring the food to the table, I won't eat. When are any of you not hungry? That's the craziest thing I've ever heard."

"Maybe it was the five-hour flight."

"Maybe you all just need an ass whooping, is what maybe it is. If you don't eat right now, then you're not going to be able to eat until dinner time, and that'll probably be late."

Osvaldo reached over with his tiny hand and took an empanada and his brothers sighed reluctantly, shaking their heads but giving in to their mother's whim. "See, you forget just how good the food is in Colombia," she said, watching pleasantly as they enjoy it. "Your mother knows stuff, you know. She's not completely out of touch."

"You don't even listen to the Beatles, mom," said Dixon.

"Why would I want to listen to a bunch of mop-haired white boys talking about holding each other's hands?" Griselda asked.

"They're not holding each other's hands," Uber protested.

"Los Lobos, that's good modern music. Los Salvajes."

"Los crap music," said Dixon.

"You're lucky you're so good looking. Don't have any good taste, but girls will love you anyway because of that cute face of yours."

"What about the Rolling Stones, or Bruce Springsteen? You have to like them?" Uber said.

"I like what I like," said Griselda. "Now come on, eat up, so we can get to the factory."

Sewing equipment decorated the warehouse they were going to make lingerie in. It was a gorgeous open-air workshop, capable of producing all the lingerie that they would need, with all the machines to produce as much as they need when they needed it.

Her boys ran ahead, running about the floor, to occupy themselves. Griselda stood next to Juan David Ochoa Vasquez, the oldest son of Fabio Ochoa Restrepo, one of the most successful businessmen in Colombia. A horse trader who bred and raised hundreds if not thousands of Paso Fino Horses.

His sons were looking for their own avenue in the market. Juan was the oldest and was already getting a foothold in the cocaine market with connections in Peru and purchasing fields in Colombia for business. "You really think you can find a market for our cocaine? A big market?"

"The biggest," she said. "We started off with ten pounds. We've done nearly two hundred pounds this year. Next year we'll be selling five hundred, if not more… I think we can get easily to a thousand pounds yearly with the only trouble I foresee is how to get it into the country. Which is why we're here."

"I love women in nightgowns and panties, don't get me wrong, but what's the plan here?"

"Our nightgowns are different. Sewn in each of them will be a host of compartments, each compartment capable of carrying one to two pounds of cocaine, without being obvious, without showing,

151

completely form fitting to the lingerie. With this business and the business in New York, we'll be able to stock planes full of young beautiful women, who will carry five to ten pounds of cocaine on their body. They'll be models for shows, or something of the sort… I'm sure you won't have a hard time auditioning beautiful women to come to America wearing gorgeous lingerie."

Juan grinned broadly. "I'm certain that such work probably does need a personal touch, huh?"

"Whatever gets it done."

"So every two months we'll cycle through ten to twenty girls with a hundred to two hundred pounds of cocaine on their person?" Juan asked.

"Pretty much. They'll come to America, come to my store, and then we'll be able to stock cash on them and send them back to Colombia. Back and forth we go, both of us getting richer than we ever should be."

Juan grinned. His lips pursed and he looked over the floor with Griselda, imagining what she imagined, outfit after outfit. The business itself would just have to be the cost of doing business, because putting money into the community was a power and protection all itself. "I like it. I like it a lot. You know, we could've set this all up without you coming down to Colombia."

"Everything is about appearances. Anette Fugo wants to take the financial success she and her husband have made in America and turn it into a success in Colombia, bringing business to Colombia. That's the goal. That's the narrative. That's what will keep us safe and keep our material from getting flagged."

"What about the ones that get flagged and caught? Some will, won't they?"

"Your side takes the fall for that. Half the line of lingerie will be traditional. They'll be shipping them over. I'll be putting them in my store. The lingerie that the women will wear will have the compartments. Meaning that once you hire them, you approach them from a different angle. The drugs will never be at the business or at my apartment. Alberto will never be at the business. We'll monitor every step we can. That's how we make this work. Also," Griselda said, her tone lowering, as her she watched her children play. "We make it clear that if they open their mouths, we murder their families, their friends, and anyone that knows their names. Do it once or twice and the girls that take these trips to come to America will never open their mouth no matter what amount of time the police threaten them with."

Juan stared down at the small, tiny woman. Not even thirty, just a little older than himself. He had thought that he wouldn't bring up the violence needed to get all of this done. The people that would have to die if someone got busted and decided to talk. He had thought she was more here as a brain for transport and that dealing with the nitty gritty would be Alberto's domain. Her directness surprised him. The casual way she suggested murdering groups of innocent people took him off guard. Made him wonder for a moment, just who he was getting into bed with. "A few people that knew your weed running business and what happened to your first husband said that you were... different."

Griselda looked up at him, his mustachioed face, sweat percolating on his brow on the hot warehouse floor, and she patted him on the back. "If I was a man, you'd say I was effective."

"I'll say that now. I think this can be a very profitable business for all of us."

"Good... then let's get to work in making it a reality."

2)

"Gracias, gracias, señora," said a woman, shaking Griselda's hand profusely. It amazed her just how much everything could change so quickly and still be so much the same. With the collapse of the currency, work was scarce, and the moment women learned that there were jobs available sewing and making clothes, a line stretched out down the road, with young and old women alike, looking for work, hoping for anything they can get. Many brought samples of things they stitched together, fixed, sewed, or more. They would make way more lingerie than she would ever sell or need for her shop, but that would all help with the taxes and more. She wasn't going to get caught out like they did Al Capone. That she was sure of.

It felt good. It offered a strange pride. A warmth of accomplishment that filled Griselda and made her excited for the future for once in her life. All day, she met with dozens of women, and hired six of them. Her sons pattered about, complaining about their boredom, hating having to be escorted by a private driver everywhere, wanting to go home to New York. That was what they kept saying. "How many weeks do we have to be here?" "How long until they're making your dumb clothes?" "Can't we just fly home to Papi Alberto now and you meet us there?" They were as adorable as they were annoying, and they were really annoying.

It took her a few days to get the women up and going on how she wanted the lingerie to be made. How to create the concealable pockets, how to pad the areas with additional fabric to make them unnoticeable, even if someone is touching them. And the women, God bless them, took to it like dogs learning to sit. Her boys, in the meantime, were spending their days at the hotel. Though the driver would pick them up and take them to their mother for dinner time, where each night they kept going to one restaurant after another, Griselda wanted to get all the good Colombian cooking she could.

She was packing up the office for the night. A day or two more, she figured, and she could take her boys home to New York. They could probably go tonight and, in truth, they probably could've gone three weeks ago. But she wanted to make sure the first shipment was ready in all its forms. That everything was working. And it felt good... it felt good to be outside of Alberto's shadow and to be listened to without thoughts of whether or not they should be asking Alberto that.

"You actually did something with yourself, huh?" a woman asked her. Griselda was looking at a box of lingerie that she was going to have Juan pick up, so he could start his end of the work and start picking up models. The stitching was perfect, the material soft, gorgeous, and concealing perfectly. They were going to have to package it flatter, not in bricks like they'd been sneaking it in, but Juan was aware of that.

Griselda opened the desk drawer nonchalantly. The women had gone home. It was just her in the office. And no one but her kids or the driver should've been in here right now. She gripped the gun she kept in the drawer and turned and looked at the woman. "Mama," she said, and suddenly felt the wind leave her wings, and the ground become unsteady, but her hand didn't leave the gun. She felt thrown back to that young girl, a teenager, bleeding and fighting for her life, and she glared at her mother. "What are you doing here?"

"Rumors carry around the ghetto," said Ana with a shrug, walking into the office, looking around and admiring it. She had aged poorly. Whether it was the drink, or drugs, or life, her face sunk in and gray hairs stuck out wildly. "When someone starts making waves, like you've been making waves, word gets around."

"Did you come for a job? Because I'm afraid we've hired everyone we need." She let go of the gun and closed the drawer.

"I came to see my daughter," said Ana.

"I'm not your daughter," said Griselda. "Haven't been since you kicked my ass and I had to run out of your home half naked in a thunderstorm."

Ana frowned; her eyes unwilling to meet Griselda's. "I regretted that the next day," said Ana.

"I truly doubt it," said Griselda. "I think you heard that I have money now, that like I always said, I would escape the shit life that you created for us, and then you regretted that you got rid of me." Griselda felt the anger boil in her blood.

"I don't care about your success. I care about you," said Ana.

"Go away madre. Vamos! I don't care about you," snarled Griselda. "I didn't have a place in your life when I was a teenager. I damn sure don't have a place in your life now that I have money and my own children."

"I'm a grandmother?" asked Ana.

"You're nothing," said Griselda. "You're nothing to anyone. You're an old dried up whore no one wants and no one will remember."

Ana stood pat. Sadness pulling at her eyes as she looked at Griselda, and at the hatred that she felt for her. "I'm sorry," said Ana, and it was the first time in Griselda's entire life she ever heard her mother say those words. "I was a broken woman then. Angry every day. Miserable. Addicted. Trying to take care of you the best that I could."

"By letting your boyfriends fuck me to their heart's content," Griselda snapped back.

"I wasn't a good mother. I know that. There's nothing I can say to take back the past. But I'm not that woman anymore. I found Christ. I live at a church —"

"You became a nun?" Griselda scoffed.

"No… I volunteer there and they let me stay there," said Ana. "I try to help people that are in my position."

"Drug addicted whores?"

"Many of them, yes," said Ana.

"Well, I'm neither drug addicted nor a whore, so I don't need you, because I've never needed you," said Griselda. "And God may forgive you, madre, but I sure the fuck don't."

"I'm not here because you need me."

"I'm not in the mood to help you, either."

"I'm here because you're my daughter, Griselda. My daughter that I haven't seen in over ten years. My daughter that I didn't know was alive or dead. And maybe it was selfishness. I wanted to see you and know that you're doing well. That I didn't ruin your life."

"Well, now you've seen me," said Griselda.

"I stay at San Jose Parrish. If you ever want to contact me."

Griselda glared at her mother, wanting to hate her, but now only feeling pity for her. Her attention, though, was broken as a clatter came downstairs. "No, no, no," said Uber.

"Si, si, si," said Dixon.

"You're loco! Batman can't beat Spiderman," said Uber.

"Can too," said Dixon.

Their feet were pattering up the stairs to their mother. Ana stood uncertainly.

The boys turned the corner and came into their mother's office and froze. "Sorry, mama!" said Dixon, grabbing his younger brothers and pulling them out of the room.

"You can go," said Griselda to her mother.

Ana stared at the boys, looking through the window to the office at them both. "They're handsome boys. You're lucky, mi hija," said Ana. "San Jose Parrish. If ever you want to see me. I'll be there."

"I won't."

Ana nodded and turned on her heels and she walked from Griselda's office and past Griselda's sons without saying another word. Griselda fought back tears, a mix of emotion running over her. She forced a smile as her sons came into the room. "Sorry, Mama, thought work was done. How was your day?" Dixon asked.

"Good…" said Griselda, wiping her eyes and grabbing the box of lingerie. "I think we're going to go home tomorrow."

"Really?"

"Really... I think we've all had enough of Colombia."

3)

The driver waited for the women, twisting a sign with Blanco Lingerie written across it, while he rocked back and forth impatiently. Paulo was a young man. When he approached Alberto Bravo and Griselda at the club, asking them if they needed anything, any help, any job, he'd do it... he didn't think he'd be in a penguin suit, wearing a black cab hat, and waiting to drive some people at the airport. But for a hundred dollars, there wasn't much he wouldn't do. Any foot in the criminal underworld was an opportunity to step-up in the business. He didn't think his start in the criminal underworld would involve being a chauffeur, but he was willing to do anything if it paid well. The town car was what made him the most nervous. The thing looked expensive. And he had no money to pay it back. But he'd made it to the airport without issue.

His instructions were simple. Hold the sign. Wait for the people to come. Take them immediately to the location he'd been given. No stops. No, anything. Drive the speed limit. Pay attention to traffic. Then take the girls to their hotel and be there to pick them up in the morning. No questions.

Juan had vetted the women. They knew what they were doing, and were being paid well for their risk. The women were beautiful. Gorgeous. The epitome of sexy. Seeing the women, Paulo felt like he might've actually gotten a reward. Three leggy and buxom brunettes and one sensual blond. Each of them dressed in long dresses and wearing winter coats for the weather outside, covering the lingerie they wore beneath.

"Ladies," said Paulo, a little too excitedly.

They followed him to the car, carry-ons in hand.

He drove, a little distractedly, trying to keep his eyes on the road, but constantly brought back to the women sitting behind him. The smell of their perfume filled the car. Shit, he was going to like a life of crime.

He drove to Manhattan, where Griselda had opened her shop. Blanco Fashions scrawled across a board. It was early. Only six in the morning. Few of the other shops, except for the small Donut and Coffee shop at the end of the street, were open. He drove down the alleyway as he was instructed and he parked the car and got out and knocked on the back door.

Griselda opened it and he went and opened the door for the models and ushered them in. "You wait outside," said Griselda. "The girls will be out soon. They'll have a box with them. You take the girls to their hotel. You take the box to this address," Griselda reached into her bra and pulled out a paper, "And then you will be at the hotel in the morning to take them back for their flight. If you don't fuck this up, there will be plenty of work for you in the future. Understand?"

"Yes, Señora," said Paulo, beaming, and going back to the car, taking one moment to get a last glimpse at the women, as they shrugged off their coats inside.

Griselda shut the door and looked at the women. She wondered how many of them Juan had vetted his own way. With life and Alberto and getting the cocaine business up and going, Griselda forgot for a while just how much she enjoyed the female form. "Welcome to America, señoritas. I believe you have some lingerie for me? Don't be shy?" She put a plain brown box on a table in front of them.

The women shared conspicuous looks with each other. Then, one by one, they removed their dresses, and then removed the colorful lingerie beneath the dresses, each of which was padded with cocaine. They really were beautiful. No one would question that they were models. "Welcome to America," she said to the girls.

She picked up the box and could feel the weight of it. At least thirty pounds, if not more, of pure uncut Colombian cocaine. It was perfect. Absolutely perfect.

Griselda stared at the women, admiring them, at their dark caramel skin, their long flowing hair, and their model-esque figures. To her side, she had envelopes, and she grabbed each one and gave each girl one of them. "Passports ladies, hand them over. In the envelopes is some money for you to enjoy yourself in New York... not too much though, don't get in trouble. Then you'll come back, dress up again, and fly home, and you'll have another envelope waiting for you at home. There's a hotel key in here, with the address written on a card. Do any of you speak English?"

"Si, un poco," said the blond.

"Good, stay with her then, and enjoy yourself in the best city in the world. Keep the cards with you in case you get lost. There's not a single taxi driver in New York that won't stop for any of you fine ladies. Show them the address on the card and they'll take you back to the hotel. If something happens... You've never heard of my shop and we've never heard of you. The driver will be at the hotel in the morning at six am to pick you up. You have a nine-thirty flight back to

Colombia. You did it ladies. Be excited. You just made more money than most Colombians make in a year. If anything happens, you're a model from Colombia here to do a show, that's all you tell anyone. Anything else... and well... You're aware of what will happen."

The women nodded grimly. They took the envelopes. And they started dressing.

Griselda's eyes fell on one woman in particular, with the longest and darkest hair. She couldn't take her eyes off of her. She reminded her so much of Gabriela. From the way her nose stuck out ever so slightly, like it had a point to the softness of her skin and the curves of her body. "What's your name?" she asked the girl.

"Luisa," she said, standing up, and fixing her breasts inside her dress.

"Ladies, take the box with you to the driver. Luisa, you stay back for a moment. Let the driver know to wait until I tell him to go." They picked up the box and the other three women walked to the door and went back outside.

"Did I do something?"

"No... What do you do in Colombia, Luisa?"

"Porque?"

"I'm interested."

Luisa shifted uncomfortably. She knew she what she was getting herself into, but it was America, and it was a year's salary for less than thirty-six hours of work, and letting Juan fuck her. She didn't know if she did something wrong. She'd hate for her story to end with a bullet in the head. She shrugged. "I do what I have to. Mi madre is sick, she has tuberculosis. I'm trying to keep my brother and baby sister in school."

"How old are you?"

"Deicinueve?"

"When I was nineteen, I was homeless. My mother had kicked me out and I had to run from an abusive boyfriend who I was either going to kill or he was going to kill me. It's hard being a young, beautiful woman in Colombia, isn't it?"

"Si, señora."

"I'd like to help you. You're free to leave, of course. The car is still waiting. But I could send him away... and you could help me and I could help you. You want to make a little more for your family?" Griselda asked, sucking her lip longingly into her mouth, as she looked at Luisa.

Luisa caught on quickly, her eyes searching Griselda's face to see if she was serious, and then her mouth trying to form words her brain wasn't catching on to. "I've never... you know... with a... with a woman before."

Griselda smiled and reached into her bra and pulled out a wad of cash. She counted out five twenties and put them on the table. "A hundred dollars goes a very long way in Colombia. Especially now. There're first times for everything, aren't there?"

Luisa nodded. "Okay... For two hundred, though?"

Griselda grinned. "How much do you charge in Colombia?"

"We're not in Colombia. We're in America," Luisa said.

Griselda liked her a lot. "Take the dress off again... slowly..."

Luisa swallowed nervously and nodded. She reached her hands up to the straps and let them slip down her arms.

Griselda went to the back door and opened it and waved the car away. She shut the door, leaned back against it, and looked at Luisa in all her naked glory. Wealth, power, and sex... How could things get any better?

4)

"Yo, Freddy... we're here at the warehouse and we haven't heard from anyone," said Eric Rossi over the phone.

"You got the drugs with you?"

"Yeah, we made the pickup. We've been radio silent for five hours. This is a lot of coke to be sitting on in one location for this long, man."

"I hear you. I hear you. Just hold the course, that's all I can say... I'll call you if I hear about anything going on... okay?"

"Yeah, yeah... fine..." Eric hung up the phone.

"What he say?" Eric's cousin asked.

"He said to wait. You better not use too much of that stuff," said Eric as he watched Teddy snort another line of coke. After about three hours into waiting, he had cut open one of the bricks and taken a gram for himself that he was cutting up and snorting. "You're going to have to pay for what you use."

Teddy snorted another line off the table and unfurled the hundred-dollar bill he was snorting it from. "They can have this hundred when I'm done with it. They leave us waiting, they can consider it part of the compensation," he laughed. "Why can't we just move it to where we usually take the pot and everything else?"

"We'll move it when we get the call to move it. Till then, we don't know where to bring it. He might be

164

looking for different people to handle breaking down the coke. Don't be a dipshit!"

"Just cause you're my cousin, doesn't mean you're above getting your ass kicked," Teddy joked. "I'm just trying to figure out something to do." Teddy's leg bounced up and down, his fingers tapping and dancing on his legs. "We're sitting on a shit ton of coke. I'm antsy man."

"Your antsy cause you're snorting so much fucking coke."

"This Peruvian shit is pretty damn good. Not as good as the Colombians, but still pretty fucking good," said Teddy.

"Don't talk about the Colombians. This is our product. We're going to make a lot of money with it. Get the idea that there's anything better out of your head."

Teddy threw up his hands. "O… Kay… Aren't we going to piss off the Colombians, though?"

"The fuck you care about some spics for? Don Giovanni gave them permission to use the territory. Now he's going to take that permission back. Easy as that. And you know what they're going to do about it? Fucking nothing, because they can't. Don Giovanni runs Manhattan."

"Alright… Just saying… hate to find ourselves in the middle of another war. You want to do a line? Since I'm going to have to pay for it anyway…" He rolled up the hundred again, and used his license to cut another line from the powder on the table. They had picked up the drugs from the cargo bay and made their way back to the warehouse the Don told them to go to. Now it was a waiting game. It was so weird not to hear anything for hours. Not a single person.

Eric shrugged. He could use a buzz, he figured. Make the time pass faster. He walked over to Teddy and plopped himself down on the couch beside him. He grabbed the hundred-dollar bill from his hand and secured it in his nostril and bent over to snort –

The door exploded open!

Eric went to reach for his gun, as men poured in with rifles secured to their shoulders, screaming, "FBI, FBI, DON'T FUCKING MOVE OR WE'LL BLOW YOUR FUCKING BRAINS OUT!"

Eric dropped his weapon, holding his hands up as Teddy joined him.

The officers rushed over as others poured in to clear the house. The officers shoved their face into the table, into the small bit of coke they had on the table. "You're under arrest!"

In Manhattan, Don Giovanni sat with his favorite dinner of Spaghetti and Sausage, when the police and men in suits poured into the restaurant. "Everyone freeze and stop what you're doing," said Roberto Colomb into a loudspeaker. "This is a police raid. We are here to issue an arrest warrant. Do not run. If you're not named in the warrant, you will be allowed to leave. Do not reach for your wallets or purses. We will be around soon to identify each person and you will be allowed to go."

Don Giovanni put his fork and knife down. Annoyance bit at his lungs as he took a deep breath. He wiped his face. And he raised his hands high in the air. "That warrant better not have a single misspelled word, or my lawyers will have your house by the end of this," said the Don.

An officer grabbed the Don's arm and he stood up and let them put his arms behind him and cinch cuffs across his thick wrists.

Roberto chuckled to himself. "What we have here," said Roberto, "Right here…" He pointed at the document as he pressed it down on the table in front of the Don. "This is an arrest warrant, issued by the New York Courts, spelling out the drugs, guns, and other illegal activity you run as a reason for your arrest. Search warrants have been issued and are being executed right now, for three warehouses, four houses, and five of your lieutenant's homes." Roberto spread the paper out to show the other warrants beneath it. "Here are the warrants for your men right there…" He nodded to the Don's security as the police took their weapons and put cuffs on them.

The Don's nostrils flared. His jaw tightened and the muscle torqued. Roberto just smiled. There was a satisfying feeling to seeing these big dangerous gangsters try to keep their façade even when they know the game is up. The fear, though, that fear that dances behind their eyes, it always made his day.

"I have no idea what you're talking about," said the Don. "I'm a minority partner in this restaurant. I have no idea what they're doing in here. And I definitely don't have lieutenants or a warehouse. I'm a small-time investor in a few good real estate deals and I support my local unions. That's all."

"Well, we'll let the courts decide all of that. Get him out of here."

Two officers pulled Don Giovanni away and Roberto watched on smugly. "We got word," said Agent Shorn, "that over a hundred pounds of cocaine seized at the one warehouse, another two hundred pounds of heroin in another. Another hundred pounds of weed in the other houses. Tons of guns. This is going to be huge, Rob... Fucking Huge! We just took down the Rossi family. We're hitting the Bonanno's next. Take the win! Put a smile on."

Roberto shook his head. "I wish I was as optimistic as you. I think this is just getting started."

5)

"I don't fucking trust them," said Griselda to Alberto. He was sitting on the couch, lines of cocaine in front of him, and she bent over and snorted a line. The burn worked its way down her nose and through her senses and tickled the back of her throat. Her head felt clear. "They didn't want anything to do with us, told us we were risking our business, threatened us –"

"When did they threaten us?" Alberto asked.

"You don't think they were threatening us?" she said. "You don't think when they tell us they'd hate to see our business and everything we built fail that that wasn't a threat?"

"Now they want our product. Don Giovanni's in prison. You've won, we've won... we can set the price, and we can –"

"They want our product because they tried to cut us out of the fucking MARKET, ALBERTO!" she yelled. "They want our product now because they lost a hundred pounds of Peruvian cocaine, and Don Giovanni was feeding that to the other families to push us out of the market, 'cause God forbid they come to the people that told them this was going to be a huge fucking market."

"It's business," said Alberto. "You shouldn't take it personally."

"I'm not taking it personally. I'm paying attention. They didn't want to work with us. But now that they're down product, down money, the Rossi family fucked, and the Bonanno's taking a hit as well. They want someone that knows what they're doing, yeah, but they came to us last, because they don't have a choice. And desperate people can become ungrateful, very fucking quick. That's what's happening here. Anything else you think is happening isn't. We have the product, we have the market, and right now, we're the source of the best cocaine out there. I'm not okay with watching as they take over the markets we spent all our time building and creating. We took cocaine from a few pounds a month, to a hundred pounds a year, to nearly a thousand pounds being moved, and they were ignoring the fucking market, and then tried to rescind our ability to sell in their neighborhoods. And let's be clear, they got snitches in their homes, because they also got their weed houses raided and lost all the product we got them for that. They fucked up. And now they want us to make it better for them. That's what it is."

"We could get up to fifteen hundred pounds if we bring them in…"

"The Italians, the Jews, the Irish, all those fucking white devils. The moment they think they can cut us out, they'll fucking cut us out, you know that, right? They're already trying to make deals with Peruvians. They're already in the process of doing whatever they can to not work with us. We let them into our process… we let them into how we do things, and we'll be fucked before you know it, Alberto. How don't you see that?"

"Then we don't let them in. We make it clear that they deal with us and us alone. And we keep them at a distance..."

"You can't keep rabid dogs at bay by telling them to stay," said Griselda. "They'll fucking attack and maul you to death the moment you turn your back. They're fucking dangerous. We'd be better off just striking first."

Alberto snorted a line of cocaine off the table. "Do you hear yourself? They control the state. You might not like it. But that's the reality of it. We can't go to war with these crime families."

"We've got men. We can get all the weapons we want..."

"They already have the weapons they want."

"Then let's leave. Let's get out of New York. Let's go set up in California. Strike with force. Let people know we're here to stay. And let's make a fuck-ton of money in the process, Alberto. Or Miami... some place without winters and snowstorms and some place with more Spanish people."

"We have our foot in New York. The amount of work needed to set up somewhere else would be insane and set us up to get fucking caught, raising red flags, and putting us in handcuffs or with bullets in our head. That's what you're doing. You're not thinking straight. That's the problem. You should leave the business to me. I started it. I've run it. Let me take care of the business aspect and you keep finding interesting avenues to get the drugs into the country. And if you see another market, we'll get into it."

"I don't like it, Alberto. This is a different game we're dealing with. We should own New York –"

"What should happen and what is happening are two different things, Griselda. Right now, they control New York. They control a large amount of the drug trade. We don't want to antagonize them."

"What is happening is that we have a product everyone wants. We control the market. So we shouldn't be so quick to give the market over to some fucking white assholes that want to take over the business."

"We're not giving it over to them," Alberto grunted. "We're bringing in partners to expand our market to bigger and better areas. We're going to be making more money and we have enough power behind us to keep us untouchable to them."

Griselda rolled her eyes and snorted derisively. Part of her knew Alberto was right, for now, but only because of the small box and picture that he was painting them into, only because he couldn't see the reality that was coming. He was dealing with what was yesterday. Not what was today.

He had become too enamored with New York. Too taken with the idea that this was the hub to grow an empire in. Too enamored with the idea that New York was a testing ground and if you could make it here, you could make it anywhere, instead of just going and making it everywhere. Griselda wanted a kingdom built by one brick of coke after another.

Griselda saw the bigger picture and a ping of resentment sat bitterly in her stomach toward Alberto.

"You handle them," she said. "You manage the fucks. If they kill you, then you'll know I was right."

Alberto laughed. "Okay, if they kill me, I'll now you were right."

6)

John R. Bartels Jr. sat in the headquarters of the New York Office of the FBI, stuffing a pipe with tobacco, and striking a match as he waited. He was an older man, his black and white hair combed over and back.

Roberto adjusted his tie, fixed his hair, and smiled with some uncertainty. He didn't know what this was about, but it was rarely good when you were called to the office to meet someone, anyone, especially after such a big bust. Did he fuck up on the warrant? Are they going to tell him that the Don turned state's evidence and they were going to let him off?

When he asked Captain Burchard what this was all about, the Captain just shrugged his shoulders. "Something about your bust, that's all he said. He's from the state department. It looks like the cases you were investigating and building for the last two years interest the White House."

"The pot and coke?"

"You've gotten about a hundred arrests, and you just took down one of the major mafia families and put a dent in another one. He's looking for someone with your exceptional record..."

"They have the BNDD for that. They have customs."

"Just go in there, answer his questions, and find out what's happening. Be cordial," said Burchard as he pushed the door open to the office and ushered Roberto into the room.

John R. Bartel seemed warm, smiling and shaking Roberto's hand as he puffed again on the pipe. He looked much more like a bureaucrat than most bureaucrats. "This is Roberto Colomb. Who you asked about?" said Captain Burchard.

"Good, good."

"What's this about?" said Roberto.

Captain Burchard shot him a look.

"Right to the point. I like it. I don't want to waste your time," said Mr. Bartel. "Nixon has launched a war on drugs and you've been one of the best foot soldiers we have in getting to the root of the problem. Customs is great at stopping the drugs from coming in. But between you and me, that's not working. The BNDD have done many operations and get a lot of drugs off the streets. But there's a heroin problem in New York."

"There are a lot of problems in New York."

"You're absolutely right. Your bust four months ago was one of the biggest seizures we've had. You're getting results. You're doing the investigations. You're building some very impressive cases. But while everyone has been focused on the mob and violence and arresting them… you've been focused on what actually could stop them… Taking down their distribution arms here at home."

"I'm doing my best, sir."

"But you're only one man…"

"The agency is doing their best," Roberto said, looking over at Captain Burchard.

"He's been running the task force successfully for two years," chirped in Captain Burchard. "We've given our full support even before Nixon made it his number one priority to get drugs off the streets. Through our efforts, we've seized over 2 tons of marijuana just last month. We caught a boat coming in with another hundred pounds of Peruvian cocaine."

"That's why I'm here," said Bartel, coughing slightly into the black sleeve of his suit jacket. "That's why I'm here. The President wants to make it clear that he's serious about drugs and he's creating the Drug Enforcement Agency. A way to bring together our Federal agencies to put a focus on ending this scourge of drugs. The drugs are coming in from every port. They're being transported from the Mexican border, from Florida, and the ports in New York. We want a more centralized attack and tracking of these things. One agency that would focus solely on the drugs coming and being sold, with broad and sweeping power to pursue criminals. Because if we try to tackle this on a state-by-state basis, we will never get a handle on it. We'll bust one dealer and they'll get replaced by another. We'll bust one drug operation and, like the Hydra of old, they'll come back with two or three other heads. But if we shut down distribution, if we capture it when it's coming in, if we get to the suppliers… Then we're playing an entirely different ballgame."

"Are you offering me a job?"

"I want you to take your task force to the DEA and expand its provisions. You'll have the full support of the United States government and your own budget, not pulled from the fields of the FBI."

"I have an enormous case being put together here," Roberto said.

"And right now, New York is one of the major epicenter hubs for pot and the resurgence of cocaine and heroin. So nothing will change right now, except more freedom and focus on what you think needs to be focused on. Take any member of your team that wants to come with you and help us end the scourge of drugs before it takes us over."

Roberto didn't think long. Being recruited into an entire other agency where he would be given broader autonomy to catch these drug pushers was not something he could pass up. "I'm in," said Roberto, taking Bartel's hand.

"Great!" said John Bartel. He puffed on his pipe one more time, and walked over to the front of the table that he was sitting at when they came in, and grabbed a folder. He walked it over to him. "Report to 10th Ave on Monday and help us win this war before it begins."

CHAPTER 9

1) 1974

Alberto handed Griselda a rolled-up fifty, and she bent forward and snorted the line of coke from a mahogany desk in their room that looked out over Central Park. They had moved for the third time in six months and this was just one of three places that they kept up, each under a different identity, each purchased by her wearing different wigs, sporting – to the best of her ability – different accents. Alberto thought it was overkill, but it was just something else she and he were disagreeing on these days.

She had strict rules. She didn't bring drugs or guns into the home she was living in, outside of personal use. The Manhattan home was their base away from operations. Nothing could ever be traced to them. She didn't even take the models anymore to her shop. Instead, having them dropped off at one of their safe houses, and transported from there to the shop, to do actual modeling of the undergarments for brochures she never sent out.

Drugs went through their safe houses occasionally, weapons as well, but with none of them under their names, or connected to them, they didn't have to worry about someone tracing things back to this home. And that meant they'd have plenty of time to escape if the worst happen. At least until Griselda decided to move again.

It was important to her to try to not move her boys too much, not that it affected anything. They didn't go to school. They spent their time with Griselda or Alberto, learning the drug business, learning how to send clandestine communications, the ins and outs of trafficking large quantities of drugs through American ports. Education, Griselda thought, that was actually worth something.

"You want to know something?" Griselda asked contemplatively, staring out over the city and the park, her body encased in the setting sun, while dusk took the city and the lights slowly came on. "I still prefer basuco," she said.

"That's cause you have a poor taste in drugs," said Alberto and laughed, before taking another snort of cocaine.

"Well, given my choice of men through my life, someone can definitely question my taste." Griselda looked over her shoulder and flashed a smile.

Alberto stayed amused, though he sensed there was a sharpness in her words. She knew of his affairs and he of hers, her slow disinterest in trying to even hide her deviancy with other women... though he would admit, when she included him in them, he didn't nearly have as much issue with it. Nonetheless, he played with the jest she tried to put into the words. "Ouch. You wound me, dear."

"Not too bad, I hope," Griselda said, taking her finger, and wiping the glass the cocaine was on, and putting the last of the residue on her gums, feeling the tingle and numbness in her mouth.

"Never..."

"How much do they want?"

"As much as we can give them."

"We can give them more than they can sell," Griselda said, hating vague platitudes and grand promises that she felt the Italians and Irish were constantly throwing out and Alberto was constantly eating up. "I want to know how much they want exactly and how much they're willing to pay."

"Three hundred and ninety-two thousand dollars for fifty pounds," said Alberto. "Up front."

She turned and shot him an evil stare that made Alberto nervous. "What is that a gram? Nine... nine and a half."

"It's ten."

"Ten a gram," she said. "We sell to all our other distributors fifteen a gram."

"Our other distributors buy five to ten pounds. They're willing to buy more, so I asked them to price out what they thought was fair. I didn't agree with anything yet."

"I don't trust the penny pinching," Griselda said. "Why three hundred and ninety-two? Why not round up? Why not make it an even four hundred thousand? Tell them two can play at their game and we'll sell them fifty pounds of cocaine for $12.83 a gram. Four hundred thousand dollars. If they don't like it, tell them they can wait on the Peruvians to figure out how to sneak it into the country without getting busted. I'm sure the next shipment will be here in a month or so."

Alberto took in Griselda admiringly. For a woman raised with no education and nothing but struggle, she had moments of brilliance. When you put a dollar sign in front of numbers, she became a veritable Einstein. Or, maybe, she overheard the conversation on the phone, and their offer, and she had the math done for her – Alberto wasn't sure about her anymore. She was always playing games. Even with him now. "I'll tell them."

"Good… 'cause they need to know we're not coming to them, they're coming to us. They don't set the price, we set the price. The moment they are allowed to set the price, like we let them do with the pot, then we're working for them. And we're not working for them anymore. Dealers are going to deal, regardless of what they get or where they get it from. So if the Italians and Irish want to go dry for a month, we can take their market. You let those fuckers know that we're not fucking peasants, we're not amateurs, we're not flies on the ass of a horse," she said angrily.

"What are you talking about?"

"Do you think that if you were one of them, if you were Alberto Bolano, bringing in a shipment of cocaine to meet their needs, they wouldn't bring you a round number, a full number. You don't see it, Alberto, and that's what's bothersome. This was an insult. This was an insult to you, to me, to what we've built and are building."

"They did the math out for what they wanted to offer."

"Keep believing that and when you turn on your car one day and it blows up, then it'll be too late to realize that they didn't even fucking respect you."

"I think the cocaine is making you paranoid, mi amor," said Alberto, getting up and walking toward her and wrapping his arms around her slightly widening waist. Most people got thin on cocaine, but it seemed to have the opposite effect on Griselda. Enhancing her vices, from her libido to her gluttony. He didn't mind, though. She was voracious in the bedroom. He looked out over the city with her. The city they did have in their grasp because of her seeing the market. Her seeing the opportunities. Her ideas to get the drugs into the city. So much of it was her. "We are going to be fine. They are playing hardball. We'll hit that fucking ball right out of the park." His hands bunched up her Chanel dress over her waist, the soft white material turning into a belt.

"We aren't giving them a fucking penny of product for less than four hundred thousand for fifty pounds," she reiterated, pressing her hands on the warm window as the streets sweltered in the summer heat.

"They're not looking to stiff us," he assured her, kissing her neck and running his hands around her chest and grabbing her breasts and squeezing them. "We're going to make a lot of money," he promised, bringing his fingers to her mouth. She opened her lips and sucked the fingers into her mouth. He pulled them out and drew them down her body and into her lace panties. "We will make sure that we get everything that is ours. And we won't lose these streets... even if we have to do what you want to do, and kill them all."

She turned to Alberto, and he kissed her lips before she could speak. She loved the passion that the cocaine brought out in him; it was like when they first met, though his manhood often needed a little more seeing to and patience before it stood full staff, thanks to the coke. "I just want what we have to be respected. I want it to be ours. It's not theirs and it can't be theirs. We can't let them take this from us. We can't let them steal our empire from underneath us. I won't let my sons end up some dead spics on the streets of New York because we didn't fucking handle these goddamn snakes the way they needed to be handled. They think they're tough with their fucking car bombs and their threats and the government officials in their pocket. They haven't truly dealt with what we could do to them."

"I'm trying to fuck you," said Alberto… "Can we talk about business later?"

"Business makes me horny," said Griselda, pressing on Alberto's head and he kissed his way down her clothed breasts, and past her slightly rounding belly, and onto the soft lace of her panties. Her sweet scent capturing his attention as he pulled them down her legs, revealing her to him. She leaned against the reinforced glass and propped a leg on the table. He scooped his hands underneath her ass and brought his mouth to her sex.

"If they try to fuck us over," Griselda moaned pleasantly, her hand playing in Alberto's hair. "We kill them. We kill all of them. Not just them, though. We make a statement, one that can't be ignored, one that says that if you fuck with us, all you love dies, and all that knows you and sides with you die with them. Let them know that there's a cost for fucking with our money and us."

Alberto laughed and shook his head. "You're loca sometimes and I love it," he said, looking up at her from between her thighs. He brought his mouth back to her and she moaned more, tossing her head against the glass with a little thump that she ignored. For minutes, he pleasured her, his hands gripping tighter to her ass, and pulling her sex closer onto his mouth, before he stood up abruptly. "Bend over," he said, grabbing her and nearly tossing her across the desk.

Griselda looked over her shoulder as Alberto worked his belt and his pants off. His excitement was obvious in the bulge that was sticking out of it. "We are going to have an empire. Not a family. Not a cartel. Not a gang," she said with an enthralled determination. "We're going to build an empire. One that will be the envy of all that come into this fucking game we're..." She paused as he thrust into her...

"We will," Alberto assured her. "An empire." His hand fell down onto her ass and the sensation erupted through her body. "An empire that you and I will rule."

Griselda grinned, liking this more aggressive Alberto. So different than he was just even minutes ago. Maybe they needed to fuck more, so he remembered where his balls were, she wondered. Maybe he wasn't feeling like enough of a man with all his putas on the side. "In the end, it has to be us that come out on top," she moaned. "It has to be you and me, Alberto. It can't be them. It has to be us."

Alberto grabbed her hair and yanked tight, pulling her up off the table, and she squealed pleasantly at the burn in the back of her head. "I promised you..." he gasped, his pulse racing, his heart beating a mile a minute, everything in him feeling like his entire body was about to burst in whatever this orgasmic bliss would be. "I promised you that I would take care of you... that we would build this empire together..." He huffed with every thrust. "And we're doing that. Four hundred thousand dollars. Not a penny less. Not a fucking penny less!" He moaned and Griselda moaned at his proclamation

Afterwards, as they dressed and Alberto said he would go to the club and meet with them and tell them the price, she stared at Alberto, watching him carefully. "Not a penny less," she reminded him.

"Not a penny less," he assured her.

2)

Fredrico Maslany dressed well in a tailored suit, a cigarette dancing from his lip, a swagger to his walk, and he dodged into a Jack's Burger Shack and made his way to the counter. Jack's Burger looked like most burger shops, with a group of young people, a jukebox, and several young teens behind the counter wearing red caps and matching aprons, with nametags. He walked up to the counter and patted his hand on the table, popping his lips, while he looked at the menu, while glancing over his shoulder at the Fed trying not to be a Fed, sitting in a booth with a t-shirt, and what was probably a diet soda, and plain burger. "What can I get for you today?" the young woman said behind the counter, her rosy cheeks and cheerful demeanor making Freddy smile.

"Well sweetcakes, I think I'll take a Jack Special With Cheese," he said, taking a moment to eye the young girl a little harder than a man his age should.

Roberto stared at Freddy, annoyed that he was making him wait. "So, sweetheart," Freddy said, stepping aside to wait for his order, "You working for school, or what?"

"Just to make some extra money, buy a car and stuff," she said, turning her attention to the next customer.

"That's good, that's good, rare these days to see kids with real work effort. Most of them running off trying to avoid this war with these stupid commies, or joining the hippies and screwing around with the Blacks. You look like a good girl, though," Freddy said.

"Um, thank you," said the girl, making a face, and trying to focus on the order.

Freddy laughed to himself, as a boy placed his cup and food down on a tray, eying him, as if he was trying to intimidate him. Freddy winked and nodded at the girl one last time and went over to the soda fountain to get himself a coke, before he walked his tray over to Roberto. "You pick the worst places to meet."

"I can always come to your club," said Roberto.

"Don't be an ass," said Freddy. "You're the big man on campus, running a new agency, taking down some major headliners. All thanks to yours truly. I should be getting a parade in my honor."

"You're swooping in like a vulture and gathering up territory and making yourself a much bigger man than when we started this arrangement." He pushed him the ashtray. "You're walking around with your own cigarettes now."

Freddy laughed. "I'm doing okay for myself. You haven't ever been fun to work with, but fuck me if you haven't become a real ass since you gave up smoking." He snubbed out his cigarette and took the burger and bit into it. Roberto watched him indignantly as the ketchup gushed around the sides of Freddy's mouth, and he enjoyed it with a passion. "So, what do you want now?"

"The Colombians. My sources say that they are responsible for nearly all the coke coming into New York right now. That little market four years ago is quickly turning into an insanely enormous market and these people have been fucking ghosts. They bounce around. They don't stay in the same place for longer than a few months. The man we have a few pictures of. The woman, Griselda Blanco, we have nothing on. The pictures we have, we're not sure it's her. We're about to hand down a lot of indictments and that means you're going to want to lie low, keep your head down, stay out of any area where they're holding the drugs, cause if you get swept up, you're either going in, or getting outed. And unless you want to end up in Bumfuck Ohio, working in a freezer, making minimum wage, you'll want to keep from being swept up."

"I understand... the problem I have with the information you want is that I can't get it. I got you the shipment, I brought down the Rossi family for you... at least put a dent in it for you. Griselda doesn't meet with any white people. Trace the coke to some niggers and spics down in the Bronx and Queens, and you'll get a clear picture of her. When I've been around Alberto, he's bitched that his wife is paranoid, that she makes him sit in safe houses and bounce around them until he's sure he's not followed before he comes home. He usually hooks up with this Puerto Rican in Brooklyn, but you probably know that shit already."

"Well, like I've been saying, that seems like it's more your problem than my problem," Roberto said. "Because I'm not asking. For a year now, we've been building a case, working with local police, and I'll be damned if I don't walk away with these fuckers after they've dumped so much cocaine into our country."

"Look, I'll see what I can do. That's the best that I can do. If you had taken my advice four years ago and started investigating these fuckers then, you would've had all the information that you needed."

Roberto nodded. He had that feeling more than once himself. But that wasn't his call. The FBI was focused on taking down the mob and saw them as smugglers and it was easier to build a case against the mob if they had the drugs on them, instead of stopping the flow of drugs. "Just do your job now and we'll all be good. Okay."

"You're more demanding than my fucking old lady, you know that, and she's a spoiled bitch."

"Well, you keep spoiling me and I'll make sure that no one looks at any of your bookmaking, or that underground casino you're running, and that escort thing as long as you keep the girls legal and consenting."

"Scouts honor. I don't deal with that type of perversion."

"Then, like always, we'll keep this a mutual and successful thing."

"Mutual..." Freddy mocked, his mouth full of another bite. "Yea, mutual! Alright... I'm gonna eat, so you can scurry on now back to your Fed buddies. And you could try to not look like a Fed for once. That shortcut hair, pressed shirt... we could all end up dead. You have me meeting in public like this."

"I offered to have you come down to the office," said Roberto.

"Here, I can say some Fed cornered me, and I told him where to stuff it. I get seen going into a Fed building and I might as well put a bullet in my own head."

Roberto got up from the booth. "I'd give you some money, but, by the look of you, you're doing well all by yourself," said Roberto.

Freddy laughed with his mouth full and waved him away as he grabbed a handful of fries and tossed them on the tray and grabbed the ketchup and started squirting it over the fries.

3)

"Agent Roberto Colomb is here sir," said Special Agent in Charge Adrian Mikkelson. Roberto was originally offered the position, but he didn't want to be taken off the street. He knew himself well enough to know that he wasn't going to be able to do the political parts of all of this. He stood in the office while a loud speaker statically filled the quiet space, while whoever was on the other end cleared his throat.

"It's good to talk to you, Agent Colomb. You've been doing one hell of a job out there, even before the establishment of the DEA. But your work has been superb over the last year," said Attorney General Edward H. Levi over the phone. The political world had moved fast. Three different attorney generals and another President. He kept waiting for this call. The call that was going to take Nixon's War on Drugs and cancel the whole thing, tossing out Nixon's legacy with all the other shit he did.

For every bit of good they did, it always seemed like it was putting band-aids over gaping wounds. He wasn't nearly sure how much of a success they've been. They had shut down several drug shipments, knocked out several distribution channels, and through officials in the AG office, gotten a lot of positive press. They largely had been left alone to their own devices. "Thank you sir," said Colomb.

"You've gotten a lot of cocaine, heroin, and pot off the street… done a lot for the war on drugs, and God knows we needed something impressive after all the shit that went down."

"I'm glad I could be of service, sir," Roberto said.

"Right now, I have orders going through the FBI and every other organization on how they're to handle cases and warrants from now on. The reason I wanted to get on the phone with you is that I want the DEA to be as successful as possible. I want you to succeed. But I want to make this clear: We will not be playing the loose games that the FBI has gotten away with. There will be no warrants without direct evidence of a crime. We need to restore the good name of our institutions and we can't have bad press happening."

"What's that mean exactly?"

"It means stick to your record. You've done amazing work and followed the law. Keep at it. Keep doing it. You're our Golden Boy out there. You're putting the biggest dent in drugs in the entire country. It will stay broad. I don't want you to worry. We're not trying to stop the good work you're doing out on the East Coast. We just want to make sure that everything follows the law of the land. That you keep you and your unit above board when it comes to the Federal side of things. You've been doing far better than most. Proper evidence brought to the courts. That's all I'm saying. Keep it up. This is a commending call to you and your team."

"Will do, sir," said Roberto, confirming to himself that this was why he didn't take the position of Special Agent in Charge. This five-minute talk was annoying him already.

"Is that all you need, Attorney General?" asked Mikkelson.

"That's all. You all keep it up out there. Keep our streets clean and our children safe."

"Thank you for the call, sir," said Mikkelson, as his hand waited over the phone to hang up the call. The line disconnected on the other end and he hit the receiver.

"I'm glad you have the job you have," said Roberto, chuckling to himself as he leaned against the small shelf and pulled a cigarette from his pocket.

"You know those things will kill you," said Mikkelson, reaching in his pocket for a lighter and tossing it to him.

"Lots of stuff in our line of work could kill us. We're taking down some of the most dangerous people on the planet. I'm sure I'm pissing plenty of people off."

"It's a sign that you are doing a good job," said Mikkelson. "Where are you on the Colombians?"

"Building the case. Finding out their network with the Italians and Irish. Operation Banshee is in full swing. We should be ready to make dozens of arrests in the next six months and put a crater sized hole in the drug supply in the entire East coast, if not the country. Cause the way I hear it, they're spreading out their shipments everywhere. And I mean everywhere. Cocaine coming into New York ports is showing up in Texas and California. Not the Peruvian shit. No. Colombian all the way through. All through two people. It's amazing. Really fucking amazing."

"You know who they are now, though, right?"

"Got names on both, pictures on one. The woman remains allusive. Every time we think we have an address, she moves. Every time we try to trace the man back to her, he's jumping from safe house to safe house after any meeting that exposes him, until he can slip from us."

"Is a woman really running the cocaine business? I didn't know Colombians were so progressive."

"She's smart, and she lets the boys play like they're in charge. But she's the only one that matters. We could take down the mob tomorrow. We could take down her husband, Alberto. If we don't know what Griselda Blanco looks like, if we don't know if that's her real name or not, if we don't arrest her with everyone else, then in weeks, she'll have an entirely new network. If you ask me... I think that's her fucking plan. It would be mine if I were in her place. Play small. Play quiet. Be the brains and be unassuming, cause you're a woman and no one pays you any mind. Then when everything goes to shit for them, walk right in and sit on the throne and declare yourself Queen."

"Then you better find out who this bitch is. We're working with four different districts. We've got the FBI, we're using a lot of resources, and people are getting antsy."

"Blame delays on the Attorney General," said Roberto, offering a sarcastically smug smile. "People are always getting antsy, until we strike, and get a ton of arrest and a ton of press, and then they're backing us the entire time."

"You really wouldn't last in my position, would you?"

"No... not for a fucking minute."

"Don't let me keep you..."

4)

"Did you drop off the money to Detective Jacobson and the three clerks at the Court House?" Griselda asked her son, Dixon. He was learning the business. Alberto had taken him under his wing, and was showing him so many things, and Griselda was having him run small jobs here and there. Griselda, wanting to keep her face as much as possible out of the public eye, found that Dixon was perfect for her deliveries to all the people that she paid off to keep the information coming and keep her family safe. He was cute, unassuming, and he knew how to play respectful well.

Alberto was hesitant when it came to approaching the police. Griselda, however, had a different idea. Especially when she was at the club and witnessed a drunken and stoned man get into a fight and nearly get himself pummeled by the security, before he pulled out a badge, and waved his side piece around like he was the boss, and told them all to back-up. She knew she found her man. Detective Jacobson had a thing for Latin women, even though he was married with three kids. And Griselda had a lot of Latin women that were eager to make as much American money as they could while they were in the country. It was a match made in heaven.

She had pictures of him with the girls, though he didn't yet know that. Pictures of him snorting coke off of several body parts. But he didn't know that either. All he knew was that if he kept her informed on what the police were doing or what they knew about her and her family, he would get a thousand dollars a week. And that, that was enough for Detective Jacobson to be completely and utterly sold on the entire idea of working for Griselda Blanco.

The first woman at the courthouse she met, she met at a salon she learned was popular with the ladies that worked near the New York Court House.

Griselda had spent most of her free time trying to learn about the justice system in America. Hiring an attorney to walk her through everything from warrants to indictments to trials and how judges are assigned. She learned the system inside and out, for which Alberto, again, thought was a waste of time. "Just better you focus on the business and the money so we can have good lawyers."

That wasn't satisfying for Griselda. As she'd come to expect from Alberto, it was always about now, now, and more now. Everything was short sighted. Nothing was on prevention. Griselda knew if they could get Don Giovanni, if they could bust all the Peruvian coke, if they could get to their shipments, as had happened on several occasions, then it was only a matter of time before something somewhere went wrong and cops were putting their name in the system. If they were going to stay free and keep making money, then they needed to be ahead of the police. There was only ever so much anyone could do before the government tried to step in and intervene. Mob Families were constantly being busted, restructured, and people that were untouchable ended up dead or in prison for the rest of their lives. Griselda wanted to avoid that fate for as long as possible.

The women were far cheaper to bribe.

It started with Lindsey.

She was a single mother, who kept that fact about herself a secret, less she risk losing her job. Griselda had a way with her. She talked about her sons. About how, "I lost my husband in a violent incident in Colombia, where I'm from. Luckily, I met a marvelous man who has taken to my sons like his own and brought us to this wonderful country. I don't know what I would've done, having to struggle to care for my boys as a single mother."

"It is hard," Lindsey said. "Luckily, Mrs. Mulberry, an older woman in my apartment building, watches Gregory while I work, for just five dollars a day. If I didn't have her, I don't know what I would do."

"How much do you make a day?"

"Well, I've been put in a supervisory role of all the secretarial work and the women in the secretarial bay that keep the entire court room running, keep the dockets up to date, and everything. So I get five dollars an hour, which is pretty good money. When I started there, I was only making three." Lindsey was thin, professional, and proud... grinning at her accomplishment. Griselda liked her.

"That's great. How old is your son?"

"Six," she said.

"My Osvaldo is seven. He had a hard time being new in school and didn't make many friends, so he's always trying to tag along with his brothers and they're often times doing what older boys do. One time they forgot him at the park. The scariest hour of my life. And I tell you I reddened those behinds so bad that they didn't sit for a week."

Lindsey laughed. "Boys... I'm glad I only have one of them."

"I'm trying to get him some English-speaking friends. You wouldn't be interested in having the boys hang out with each other, would you?"

Lindsey, like so many others would be in their lives, was taken by Griselda. By her calmness. By her smooth talking. The way she seemed to stare so caringly and intently into her eyes. "I think Leo would like that a lot."

Lindsey couldn't believe Griselda's penthouse. She'd never seen such luxury. "I've never seen anything so amazing," she proclaimed. "This is just... you live here?"

"I definitely don't work here," said Griselda. "We're likely moving soon. Alberto's business is doing so well. He likes to keep upgrading us."

Osvaldo peeked behind his mother's legs. "Hello," said Osvaldo.

"Hello," said Gregory.

Griselda cleared her throat and Osvaldo moved himself in front of his mother's legs. "I have a lot of toys. You want to check them out and play?" he asked.

Gregory looked up at his mother, strands of dusty brown hair covering his greenish pale eyes. "Go 'head..."

Soon, the boys were off running to Osvaldo's room.

Griselda wanted to feel her out. Wait for the opportunity. Wait until her hooks were in so tight that to turn her down would hurt her. After the playdate went well, they started doing things together more frequently. Griselda got her dressed up in some lingerie for a date she had with a lawyer. She treated her out to lunch on several occasions. But with all the time she spent with her, she couldn't find an in that felt right.

That was until two tragedies struck in a row for Lindsey that that window Griselda waited for opened up. When Mrs. Mulberry didn't notice that Gregory got a splinter and it got infected and Lindsey had to race him to the hospital and pay a lot of money out of pocket to keep him from losing his finger, she called Griselda from the hospital in a mess. Sobbing into the phone.

And Griselda went down to the hospital and sat with her and Gregory for hours. It was close. It was almost right. Griselda could feel it. Then it happened. Lindsey's car broke down a week and a half later. She called Griselda from a pay phone, in tears once more, begging her for any help, cause she didn't have any money for a cab. It was perfect. There couldn't be anything more perfect. Griselda smiled so widely her cheeks hurt.

"It's going to be fine. I'll close the shop and I'll be right over. Where are you?"

Fifteen minutes later, she was pulling up to pick her up.

"Did you really have to close your store? I feel so guilty now. I'm costing you money."

"It's no problem. No one comes that early in the morning for lingerie anyway," Griselda said.

"You're a good friend."

"It's really no big deal. I really value our friendship. You've been great to have in my life."

"Thank you," said Lindsey. "You've been great to have in mine. I don't know what I'm going to do. I don't have a car now. Gonna have to take the subway everywhere. I don't get it. You know, I work hard, I take care of my son. There are women out there in my situation that are on welfare. Here I'm trying to do the right thing, and nothing: The world just fucking hates me."

"The world doesn't hate you," said Griselda.

"It definitely doesn't like me," said Lindsey.

"You know, if you need money, I could help you out. It's no big deal."

"I couldn't ask that," said Lindsey.

"You could do me a favor."

Lindsey looked at her with a piqued interest. "What?"

Griselda reached into her bra and pulled out two thousand dollars and dropped it into Lindsey's lap. "My husband's work has some questionable components. Occasionally, he'll try to avoid taxes on some transports. I tell him I hate it. But you wouldn't imagine the savings we get when we can bring in my clothes or stuff without having to pay the tariffs on imports. If anything would come in on the dockets, such as a subpoena, or the holding of a grand jury and an indictment... giving me a heads up would be very gracious. If not, that's fine. You can forget I ever asked."

Lindsey looked at the money in her lap. It was more money than she made in two months. She could get a new car. She could get a new place to stay. She could do so much with it. And it wasn't like she was asking her to do something horrible. Hell, it was probably barely illegal. If it was illegal at all.

"Just importing and exporting things."

"We're not murderers," Griselda laughed.

"I know that."

"If you're uncomfortable, forget I asked. I just want to protect my family, is all. The American legal system is something that when you know what's happening ahead of time, you can get ahead of things with lawyers and everything. But I see you're nervous about it... so forget it."

"No, no, no," said Lindsey, holding the money tight to her breasts. "No... I mean, I think it's horrible that they would target a successful immigrant family for what probably every business does when they can

196

get away with it. I will definitely have my eye out. But you know there are different courts for several things."

"Do you know any women working in them?"

"I do," Lindsey said.

"That's not a onetime payment," said Griselda. "I can get you five hundred a month and anyone you bring me that's in your position, two hundred and fifty a month, for that information."

Griselda pulled up to the courthouse. "Thank you," said Lindsey. "You have no idea how helpful this will be."

"Hopefully, you'll never need to pick up that phone and say anything, and I just get to help a friend."

Lindsey smiled and nodded and slid the money into her purse and got out of the car.

4)

Roberto sat in the car with two other men on a cold fall day, while they watched for Alberto Bravo to come from the safe house. They had three different agencies on him. Louis Capaldi and Eric Shorn were two of the first men Roberto brought over from the FBI to the DEA with him. He trusted them sometimes more than he trusted his own wife. But for all their hard work and good maneuvering, they weren't yet clear, even a year in, to what they were doing differently than when they were working for the FBI.

That was, by and large, the major challenge that he faced with everyone he worked with. The goals of those agencies were often to catch big headlines by taking down big named people. The BNDD and customs wanted to catch drugs coming into the country. This wasn't about big names, even though there were definitely a lot of them entangled in this operation. It wasn't about headlines or catching a huge amount of drugs. Even though that was why it was so easy to recruit so many agencies for Operation Banshee. There were a lot of big name people. But the DEA's goal was different. Yeah, they, like every organization, wanted to grab some headlines. But their goal wasn't just to build the biggest case possible against the biggest name possible. Their goal was to disrupt the very flow at the source. Shut down suppliers working inside the United States. The mob, at the end of the day, worked largely as distributors and low-level dealers, and though they would get caught in the same broad net, the goal wasn't to bust up organized crime. That was a side-effect of what they were doing now. What they needed was to catch Alberto Bravo and his wife.

They had been sitting on Alberto for the last three days after his meeting with the restored Rossi family. They had another team on another side of the building. He was so casual since his meeting. It was down to a pattern. Safe house one. Some friends would stop by and at night Allaina Castiano had visited him twice, once overnight, where they did some drugs, and had sex a lot. He didn't call his wife once. Whatever Griselda understood about the government's procedures was keeping her off their radar better than some of the biggest gangsters in this country. How this woman seemed to stay one step ahead of them was frustrating as hell.

A black Cadillac pulled up to the door and Alberto came out with Allaina, a joint bouncing on his lips, and Allaina under his arm. He opened the back door and helped her into the car, and then ran around the other side and got into the car. They waited for the car to go and they followed it for over an hour deep into the Bronx. "Fucking hell... How many safe houses does this guy have?" moaned Capaldi.

Roberto's men had mapped out at least four different safe houses that he traveled to before he'd often disappear. But Roberto was determined. "Let's put the Bronx PD on him to sit on him."

"We could just grab him, bring him in, put him under pressure... We got him on a bunch of crimes... and he has no loyalty to any of the Italians. He'll flip in an instance."

"He'll flip in an instance on them, because his wife will be out of the country the moment we pick him up, and they'll still have their smuggling operation going. Like I said, we're not here to bust the mob. That's the FBI's big goal, that's what they'll do," he said with a little bit of exasperation.

"We're here to stop the drugs," said Capaldi, "I get it."

"Good," Roberto said. "Let's not lose track of that. I want the woman. From everything that I've heard, he plays connect, he makes the deals, but she's the one that's the mind behind getting all the drugs into the country."

"We got it..." said Agent Shorn.

"We're going to take them all down."

5) 1975

The phone was ringing endlessly in Griselda's beautiful penthouse in Queens. She had moved again, feeling like she was showcasing too much of her wealth in Manhattan and drawing the wrong attention. Her boys were stopped three times separately and questioned what they were doing in the neighborhood.

Alberto was pulled over a half dozen times, luckily he hadn't had anything on him when it happened. Those cops, though. Those cops. She wanted to kill them. But she knew that would draw too much attention... for now. But she'd remember them.

Griselda liked Queens. She liked the name. She liked the location. Fuck, she liked the Spanish flare that was in so many of the neighborhoods. Most importantly, she liked that she could get some decent empanadas that actually tasted like Spanish people made them and knew what they were doing.

The best part, of course, was that they didn't draw attention here.

She had hired some help around the house, but they were out running errands for her as she often had them do, and Alberto was off seeing that the latest shipment was coming in safe and sound with Dixon with him. This was going to be their biggest year. They had been making moves all year since the beginning of 75, going from ten million a month, to thirty million a month, to thirty-five, to now, in April, they were bringing in enough cocaine to easily make forty million dollars. It felt good to be single-handedly creating a massive cocaine craze throughout the U.S. There were news reports about it. Scare tactics. Danger, danger, and she loved watching it. Loved more to smoke her basuco while watching it. Americans would make propaganda on anything and, of course, her cocaine was no different.

None of it was working. If anything, all these scare tactics were just making people more hyped. More wanting. Asking for it. "That stuff I heard on the news." And they were getting rich off of it. So much so, they couldn't wash it all. The money they couldn't wash was in warehouses, businesses, in safe houses, just about anywhere you could hide the money.

They say if you can make it in New York, you can make it anywhere. Griselda always thought that was the dumbest shit ever. None of the putas she had met here would last a week in the slums of Colombia that she grew up in. They'd be robbed, drugged, and left in a ditch with their tongues pulled through their slit throats. The Dons and Godfathers, all high on the hog after *The Godfather* came out, thinking they were the next Michael Corleone. But they weren't. They weren't even close. They were nothing like that gorgeous man, Al Pacino. They were wannabes. Playing by rules in a game that had no rules.

Taking one last hit from her custom-made pipe, having her basuco shipped in with the models, so she could have her drug of choice. Griselda moaned loudly as she inhaled. She had the pipe made with its own small thin steel platform, so that she could spread the basuco on it and heat it and smoke it with ease. But the ringing phone was disrupting this perfect high. "What is it Goddammit?"

"The cops are coming! They're coming soon, Madrina!" a voice on the other end said urgently. It was Detective Jacobson. "You and Alberto got to get out of there. They just got the indictments at the grand jury. They are going to be sending cops to your place immediately. If they aren't already in route."

"Fuck!" she screamed, slamming the phone down. The phone started ringing again and she figured it was Lindsey or the other girls at the courthouses, someone calling to tell her what she now already knew. That this fun time in America was ending if she didn't move fast. She had no interest in the long, drawn-out affair of trials and hearings and seizures, or her children being sent to foster care or deported back to Brazil... To what? An orphanage. That wasn't going to happen.

She had worried this day would come. Worried that they weren't moving fast enough to get themselves so rooted that the government couldn't pull them out. They should've been doing thirty to forty million a month last year, had the money up to eighty million a month or more now. But no... Alberto kept urging caution. Slow and steady. The market wasn't ready for it. She wondered why she even listened to him. It was her ideas to spread the money out into club investments and housing and everything else that they bought. Her ideas that kept everything going. All he was, all he could do, was be the labor and the face... And he wasn't that good of a face anymore.

What was their crime? Getting people what they wanted. Buying and selling products. Living the American dream. This was America, though, she thought. They couldn't let the brown people get ahead of the whites, even when it came to crime. This was the one thing she was certain about.

Griselda knew it would come. She planned for all of this. Alberto kept calling her crazy, kept complaining about all the security measures she kept having him do. Even when he saw the cops following him, tracking him, he felt like it wasn't a big deal. He thought they were untouchable. She was the one that THOUGHT, actually thought. That actually used her brain. Now it was her brains, her planning, and her escape that were going to keep them from prison, while everyone else goes down. They were going to lose a lot of money, but luckily they had a lot of money to lose.

"Uber… Osvaldo!" she screamed, coming out of her office.

Uber and Osvaldo came from their rooms. "Dress and grab your bags, now mi hijos! We must go. Like we planned. Like we planned! Vamanos!"

They snapped to attention, running back into their rooms and dressing as quick as they could. She had run these drills with them, preparing them for this day to the point of exhaustion. She wanted them to be able to get their stuff and get ready in the middle of the night in under three minutes. They, like her, kept go-bags with clothes and things they wanted to take with them when this day was to come. Osvaldo had toys that he loved and when he took them out of the bag to play with them, he always put them back. Uber wasn't nearly as sentimental. He had clothes, knowing his mother would buy him whatever they needed to replace afterwards once they landed wherever they were going and got the money flowing again.

Dressed and with their bags, they soon joined their mother.

Grabbing her go-bag she kept in the closet and Alberto and Dixon's as well, she made her way out of the building, with her children in tow, and through the back exit in case she hadn't beaten the police out the front.

There was something majestic about the New York streets. Something she had forgotten about after being here for so many years. But worried that she might never get to see it again, the cement jungle that had been her home, it felt novel once more. The swell of machines, the rise of building that reached high into the sky. Cement and metal that had replaced the dirt and clay she grew up around. But now they'd have to go back. They didn't have a choice. There was only escape.

She made her way a few blocks from the house, her son Uber, grabbing Dixon's bag for her, as she struggled to haul three bags through the street. "Gracias, Uber," she said.

When she was sure she was far away from the apartment, far enough not to draw the attention of police, she climbed herself into a phone booth and recited Alberto's car phone number in her head before dialing the number rapidly. The car phone was itself another thing that Alberto scoffed at. And another thing that was going to protect his freedom. "Why would I want people to call me when I'm in the car?" he had moaned when she suggested he have one put in. "I'll be driving. I don't need some bulky fucking phone around. Fucking drive into a wall or something trying to answer it." It was just another thing she was right about.

"Hola?" he said hesitatingly, a little surprised at someone actually using the phone.

"Do you have Dixon with you?"

"Si, si... why?"

"We're busted. The fucking cops are onto us. We got to go and we got to fucking go now! I've got your go-bags, I've got money, I've got Uber and Osvaldo and I'm heading to Newark now!"

"What do you mean?"

"What do you mean, what do I mean, Alberto? They've indicted us. The fucking cops, or the feds, or whatever fucking group that wants to put us behind bars has indicted us. They're fucking trying to arrest us. We've got to get the fuck out of this country. We got to get back to Colombia, or we're going to go to prison."

"Are you sure?"

"Yes, I'm fucking sure. Alberto, this isn't the time to second guess. I bet it was those fucking wops or those mick bastards. This is why I told you never to come right home from meeting with them. 'Cause they're organizations are full of nothing but snitches and cowards. And they're always being watched by the fucking cops. This is someone trying to make a move, so they can get the territory, and try to swarm it with the Peruvian bullshit," she snapped into the phone. "Just get to the fucking airport and let's get the fuck out of the country now!"

Alberto was silent on the other end. Probably thinking about whether or not she was right all this time. Ever since they lifted their heads up into this chaotic world and started bringing the Irish and Italians into the cocaine trade, eyes were looking their way. And maybe they should've killed all of them, every one of them, cleared the way. He didn't want to start such a big war.

Alberto was a coward, she thought bitterly. They could've ruled New York. Been the Queen and King of New York. Now they were going to be exiles.

"I'm going to kill whoever it was."

"It doesn't matter who it was. It matters that we get to Newark and we get on a plane and get the fuck out of the states. And it matters that we do this right the fuck now!" she screamed into the phone. How did she let herself fall for such a thick headed and stupid man? It had to be his good looks. His money. His power. That thin, fit physique, that beautiful head of hair, and that mustache… Okay, she couldn't be all that mad at him. "I'll see you in Newark, or I'll see you in Colombia. One way or another, I'll see you soon, my love." She hung up the phone and stepped from the booth.

Waving down a cab was easy. Dressed in Chanel and with a slender Rolex dangling listlessly on her wrist and wearing a pillbox hat, cabs never hesitated to stop for her.

Having the cabby pop the trunk, she threw the luggage in and then settled herself and her kids into the back as a cop car whooshed by, its lights blaring, the alarm whirring with a fervent cry for justice, and she thought certainly for her. "I need to go to Newark."

"Jersey... get the fuck out of here with that bullshit. I don't go to Jersey," the thick-skinned Italian said.

Her sons looked nervously. They knew their mother's temper. They'd witnessed their mother on more than one occasion shoot people, beat them with a gun, or threaten to do ungodly and horrible things to them and their families. Most of the time, those things were about money, about business. This guy was risking her freedom and that of her children. Uber grabbed his mother's arm and squeezed it tight, urging her not to overreact.

Griselda grimaced at him, then nodded, while the cabby looked at her disinterestedly, waiting for her to leave or give a different location. He had a large red nose and red cheeks and was chewing on a toothpick. "Well lady, you getting out, or you got another location?"

She fought back that violent urge, her jaw twinging and a muscle moving in her round face as she clenched her teeth. Pulling her wallet out, the man sat pat, and she counted out five hundred dollars and shoved it into the front seat.

"I need to go to Newark. Turn off your radio. Turn off the fucking meter. Forget you're driving to Jersey. And drive me and my children to Newark. Don't say a fucking word or ask a fucking question. And I'll give you another five hundred when you get there."

The driver eyed the money in the woman's hand, his fingers itching to take it. A thousand dollars for an hour and a half of his time? That was a lot of money. He would push the cab there if he had to. He took the money and counted it, looking back at the kids who knew that this might be the last decision that he ever made, if he made the wrong one, and he reached forward and shut off the dispatch to his cab and flipped off the light. "Whatever you say, lady. Whatever you say. You need to me to stop anywhere else? Your kids want some food for your flight? What do you need, darling?" He stuffed the money into his pocket.

PART 5
BECOMING A QUEEN

CHAPTER 10

1) 1975

"Where is Alberto?" Griselda asked, knowing the answer before the words left her mouth.

Since they got back into Colombia and had to leave behind their life in America, Alberto had made himself even more scarce than he had been before. She knew about the affairs in America. The Puerto Rican, the Dominican putas, all of them that liked the nice stuff he bought them, and the drugs he gave them, which made his sad, pathetic cock worth it for them. It was why she moaned so pleasantly when she was with him when they first started dating, she thought bitterly.

The women in America, though, were nothing more than playthings for him to kill time with as he hopped from safe house to safe house. Besides, she was having her fun too, and she couldn't begrudge him too much. He always came home.

But in Colombia it was different. They weren't running from the cops. They weren't trying to keep the cops from finding them. Colombian police were far more understanding and far easier to bribe and threaten. The Cartel they worked with kept them in control.

They had only been back a few months in Colombia and it seemed like he was always running off and staying gone for days on end once more. She had him followed and knew where he was going. That he had taken up a second residence. That he had another woman. At least when he did it in America, it was under the rouge of shaking off the police that might have been following him, and likely were. Now, however, she stared at her sons, hoping they had an answer, and knowing they didn't. Knowing that he was at the other residence, fucking some puta.

Dixon shrugged his shoulders and she seethed.

What little feelings Griselda had for Alberto were disappearing by the day. They had become more and more business partners than life partners, and even the business end of things wasn't nearly as solid anymore. And that's what bothered her the most. It was one thing for him to take lovers. To not be around. She could play that game too. But he was fucking with the money now. That's what she wanted to talk about, needed to talk about.

The home in Colombia was bigger than anything they had in New York. American dollars were going a very long way in Colombia as inflation continued to take hold. She lived in a near mansion. Not so big that it would draw too much attention, but they had ample yard, televisions in every room, jacuzzi tubs, and more. She walked across the marble floors, her heels clacking with every step, as she made her way to her office. She enjoyed having an office. Especially this one. It felt special. Lined with mahogany and oak, with a view out across their large yard. She grabbed the phone and reached into her desk drawer and pulled out a piece of paper with a number written on it.

She dialed angrily. Slamming her fingers into the numbers, she pressed the receiver to her ear and waited for him to pick up.

"Who is this?"

"Your wife," said Griselda.

"How did you…?" He stopped himself, knowing her capabilities and not wanting to waste time with the details. "What do you want Griselda, that couldn't wait until I get back?"

"Don't bother coming back," said Griselda. "Enjoy your fucking whores. We can make this all about business."

"Really Griselda? Don't act all high and mighty darling, we all play around."

"Play and moving away from home are two different things. I shipped three hundred pounds of coke through the clothing line to our distributor. The money should've come to you by now. Why am I only seeing a few hundred thousand dollars?"

"Because that's what I sent you. Some money for you," he said. "I'll take care of the rest. I've never left you wanting."

"We've always split it fifty-fifty."

"In America, that was necessary. In Colombia, not so much."

"It's still my money."

"It's my money. It's my connections. You wouldn't even be in this business if it wasn't for me."

They had millions stored away and they were making millions more, going through the transport side of things, still feeding their dealers – her dealers and suppliers and her transport routes – with drugs. It was a simple request, she thought. "I'm the one who built the network. I'm the one who continues to figure out ways to get the drugs through customs. I'm the one that is making any of this possible."

"Don't be a puta," he said. Don't be a puta? Was he really going to say that to her? Was he going to pretend like he would have any success beyond his small bits of trafficking here and there, making hundreds of thousands of dollars instead of the tens of millions that she made the business out to be? "This is my business. You are my wife. Be happy that I give you any of the money." He hung up the phone and she slammed down her phone so hard her children scattered back to their rooms.

Griselda tossed herself down onto the leather chair. He wouldn't treat her like this. She wouldn't allow it. Nor, however, was she going to risk everything until she had things in place. Griselda picked up the phone and dialed another number. "Dario... Darling..." she cooed. Dario Sepulveda was a respectable man, his brother a hitman, him a purveyor of tools, names, people... a fixer who knew everyone.

One of the few men, Griselda, was always happy to hear on the other line. "What can I do for you, Madrina?" he asked. His sweet voice made the hair on her arms stand on end.

"I'm throwing a party. I need all the people you can get. There'll be drugs, alcohol, and all the women that can be enjoyed... You know... one of my parties."

Dario laughed into the phone. "Sounds good, Madrina."

"I like it when you call me that," said Griselda.

"You are La Madrina," he said. "The Godfather has nothing on what you can do."

"You flatter me."

"I think Fabio Ochoa is in town after selling some horses. I know Juan will be there, because he wouldn't disrespect you like that with all the money you're making him."

"He likes all the pussy that's at my parties as well," she laughed.

"That too."

"There's something I'd like to discuss with you… in person…"

"Well, I'll be at the party as well," said Dario."

"I look forward to it."

2)

Four months back in Colombia and Dixon and Uber weren't sure how they felt about being back. Osvaldo cried a lot but had stopped that, and was getting used to Colombia the same way he got used to America. They did, however, like helping their mother set-up the parties and at fourteen and thirteen, they enjoyed the stuff they got to see at the parties. It wasn't like Griselda forced them away into their rooms.

Dixon picked up the alcohol for his mother. The store owner knew Dixon and, more importantly, knew Griselda, and though he was only fourteen, didn't hesitate to hand him over the boxes of alcohol for him and his brother to carry. Nor did the police stop them as they drove by, seeing the two young men, except to roll down their window and say, "Would you like a ride back home?"

Uber and Dixon got into the police car together. The officer in front tipped a cap to them. "You let your

214

mother know that Pilo Rodriguez brought you all home safe and sound," he said with a smile.

Dixon nodded. That was one thing he liked about Colombia more than he liked America. People respected and feared his mother here, more even than they did Alberto, and in turn, they respected them. In fact, it was always tell your mother this, tell your mother that, "let me help you out, wouldn't want your mother to think that I saw you all needed help and didn't help you."

Uber got on the phone. He hated doing that. But Griselda thought his shyness was a weakness that he needed to overcome, and it started with him making all the calls that she needed made to people. Going up and asking people for things. She wasn't going to have some "shy little boy" trying to run her empire when he got older. They were gracious the moment they heard his mother's name. "Si, si, we've got everything ready and we'll have all the food at the house at seven. Let your mother know. We have everything handled. It's all good."

Osvaldo... Osvaldo stayed in front of the television, watching a Colombian show he felt was very inferior to what he was watching in America. He loved American television. He loved *The Wonderful World of Disney*, and the *Six Million Dollar Man*, which his mother would laugh at, saying, "We have tens of millions and we can't get any of that done." She'd smile and rub his head. With his brothers they'd watch *M.A.S.H*, *Happy Days*, *Good Times*, and *Barnaby Jones,* they're favorite. The one show he and his brothers absolutely loved and he missed so much was *Kung Fu,* though his brothers would always beat him up after watching it together. He wanted to be back in America, and he couldn't wait until they got back there. *Yo Y Tu* and *Sabados Felices* just weren't the same as American television. And the American television they got, *It Takes A Thief, Bewitched,* was all voiced over... and voiced over poorly. There was just so much less on. But he tried to make do while everyone else was running errands and he had nothing else to do.

For the people that were coming, getting invited to a Griselda Blanco party was like being told that you made it. At least in the circles that would get the invitations. Businessmen came for the drugs and women and for some opportunities to help her "invest" her money in ventures that would secure some of her capital from investigation and other such issues. Women came knowing they could snag a man or the more adventurous among them, a woman, for themselves. The dealers, the criminals, the underworld all came because outside of the few people that were making more money than her that would also be there, Griselda Blanco and Alberto Bravo had set the bar for what was possible in the drug world, and if you wanted in the business in any real way that wasn't selling bags here or there, then you needed to make friends and get known. Griselda made that possible to do safe and friendly.

The parties for Griselda were something else entirely.

To most, they saw them as bacchanals. A woman with a lot of money and power doing what she wanted and having fun with it. But Griselda understood something that none of them understood… especially not Alberto.

The person they talk to. The person who keeps them abreast of the business. The person who feeds them ideas and listens to their problems. That's the person who everyone is going to see as in charge. The person who is front and center with those who matter most will carry the power. They were her way of saying that she was in charge. That she was the one that was the brains of the operation. She was the one organizing things and making things happen. Whether it was getting people together, or getting drugs across the border. It was her. Alberto was, if anything, a hardworking mule, doing the heavy lifting, staying in front of people for deals, and the first to get arrested or killed if need be.

By the time night had come, her mansion was lit up and fancy cars decorated her large driveway. There were ushers at the door. And there was Griselda, waiting to greet people. Specifically, one person.

"Don Fabio," she cried, wrapping her arms are the thick body of Fabio Ochoa Restrepo – Don Fabio to those in the know. He was a fat man, bald, with a penchant for white suits that hugged his body in all the right ways. To the outside world, he was a brilliant horse breeder with a passion for Paso Fino horses. A legitimate businessman with tons of legitimate business ventures. An upstanding member of Colombian society. To those in the know, Don Fabio was the head of the Ochoa family, for whom his sons managed the biggest cocaine empire the world had yet to fully understand. She let go of him and tilted her head to his oldest son, who came in with a cigarette dancing on his lips. "Juan, darling, a pleasure... a while... I love our silence!" she laughed as she hugged him.

"Who's that?" Don Fabio asked.

"If I don't hear from you, then you're getting paid, and if you're not hearing from me, it means I got the drugs, and that means everything is running on schedule exactly as it should. The women, the drugs, the drinks, the food, all to the right Juan."

"You know me well, Griselda," he said, nodding his head and taking his leave.

"Splendid party as ever, Griselda," Don Fabio said, taking off his jacket. With a wave of her hand, someone was there to take his jacket and put it up. "Where's Bravo?"

"Not working as always. Having his fun. Enjoying the money he makes off your product. I guess we both do that, though."

"I guess you do."

"How's your youngest?"

"Great, as always. Making a trip to New York."

"I want to get back to America."

"Entiendo... We want you back in America. There's a growing market in Miami, and one of the people running it is at your party."

"Really?" Griselda asked, with a knowing raise of the brow.

Don Fabio pointed a chubby finger at a young chubby boy named Pablo, who stood brazenly flirting with some scantily clad girls that always made their way to Griselda's parties. "I'm guessing you already knew that."

"I did. But I'm amazed at how quickly you were able to hear about it. Is it cause he killed Fabio Restrepo and you were worried it was you for a moment?"

"I never worry if it's going to be me. If someone even thinks about killing me, they ought to just kill themselves first."

"I'm sure I don't have to tell you to have all the fun you want tonight, Don Fabio."

"No, no, you don't need to tell me… we'll talk later."

"Si."

Griselda watched as Don Fabio joined his son, putting a hand on his shoulder, and admiring the woman he was talking to.

With that out of the way, with honors and respects paid, she could get to work.

Pablo Escobar wasn't here by accident. She went out of her way to make sure he was aware of the party and that he should come to it. Luckily, he had a penchant for parties. And he needed the connections more than ever, having just assassinated the small-time drug exporter Fabio Restrepo and taken his business from him. He was here, like many that showed up, trying to court his own deal with the Ochoa family.

Griselda liked the young man. Brutal for the sake of brutal. She had him researched the moment she heard of the demise of the idiotic Restrepo. "You, young man," she said to Pablo. He immediately stood at attention, pushing the girls away and coming over to her, as she crooked a finger in his direction.

"Si, Madrina. What can I do for you?"

"Is it true that you murdered Diego Echavarria even after they paid you fifty thousand dollars?" Pablo sucked his lower lip into his mouth and looked around nervously.

"Um… is it safe to talk so much in the open?"

Griselda made a face, amused that he'd be concerned about saying something in her home. "What's said in mi casa, stays in mi casa. No worries. No one here will ever speak a word of what they hear."

"Si, Madrina," Pablo nodded and smiled. "The son of a bitch spit on me and called me a dog. I showed him what a dog can do."

Griselda laughed loudly and threw her hands on Pablo's shoulders and lower her head to his. She loved it. "That's good. That's very good," she said excitedly. "I did the same thing when I was eleven. I had kidnapped this kid with some friends. He was rich and his parents refused to pay us the money we wanted. It was cheap too. I think ten thousand dollars. I was poor back then and this kid was whining and complaining and whimpering. Just so fucking annoying. So when his family didn't pay up. My cohorts wanted to get rid of him, but none of them wanted to be the one to pull the trigger. So they gave me the gun. I shot him and buried his body in a hole, and as far as I know, they've never found him." She cackled like a witch, and Pablo joined her in laughter. Not uneasy laughter either. Not some fearful, scared, or concerned better go along type release. He loved the story as much as she loved telling it.

"What can I do for you, Madrina?"

"Do for me? It's what we can do for each other, Pablo. You just took over Fabio Restrepo's business, did you not?"

"Si."

"He ships a lot of cocaine into the port of Miami?"

"Si."

"Tell me about Miami?"

Pablo rolled his lips and he thought for a moment. "Should I not talk to Alberto about that?"

"Look at me, Pablo," she said, suddenly stern, and Pablo stood upright and stared at her as he would his mother when she got that tone with him. She looked into his dark brown eyes. "How much money are you making?"

"I'm doing well."

"How much?"

"About a hundred thousand dollars this month?"

"I made a million dollars today. Today. This month I'll make thirty million. Had I not gotten kicked out of fucking New York, we would've probably been up to eighty-three million dollars a month already. Do you know what eighty-three million dollars a month means?"

"No, I don't. What does it mean?"

"It means you're a billionaire. If you make eighty-three billion dollars a month, you're a fucking billionaire. And we were close. Now tell me about Miami." Griselda put an arm over his shoulder and pulled him to the side and over to a table.

"Fabio thought small," he said, sitting close to her, as a live band played across the room. "He was shipping about fifty kilos a month over to America. He has no major distribution network. Largely, he was a

221

feeding one big fucking dealer. Such a fucking waste for the effort. Miami is ripe, like a fucking virgin with three shots of tequila and a line of coke. Just waiting for the taking. I'm hoping to get it up to two hundred kilos this year."

"Just two hundred?"

"We all have to start somewhere, Madrina. There are a lot of networks to build in Miami. A lot of work that has to be done."

"And how big do you want to be?"

"Truthfully?"

"Why would I want you to lie to me?"

"With no disrespect, I want the whole fucking world!"

Griselda smiled at this ambitious decree. "I see you've met Pablo," said a voice suddenly from behind her. Dario. She would recognize that deep, soft, masculine tone anywhere. She startled for a second and calmed down, wrapping her arm over her shoulder and around his head. "Pablo, it's nice to see you," Dario said, while in this awkward headlock, his cheek pressed against Griselda's. He reached around her arm pit to grab his hand and shake it.

"Dario, thank you for the invite. It is being very illuminating. Do you want me to go?"

"I do have business to talk with Dario," said Griselda. "But I like your ambition. Here's what I want you to do," said Griselda, signaling for a young woman whose eye she caught from across the room to come over. "Take this girl. Have some fun with her," said Griselda, barely acknowledging the girl as she came over. "Then expect to hear from me soon, okay? Drink, get high, fuck, and we'll see if I can help you conquer the world."

Pablo nodded and stood up and the woman came to his side. Thin, wearing a tight top, with no bra, her nipples pressing through the sheer material. He threw an arm over her and nodded once more at Griselda.

Dario spun around and took Pablo's seat. "The party seems to be a great success," he said.

"Thanks to you."

"People would've come, regardless. You hear what they call you, La Madrina. You have their respect."

"Where does Alberto's respect level rank?"

"Far from yours. Why?"

"Just asking."

3)

"Seven million fucking dollars!" she screamed so loud it felt like her throat was going to rupture. "Where is the seven million dollars?"

"Calm down," said Alberto over the phone. "I've paid for everything, have I not? Are you wanting for anything? Do you not have money?"

"You motherfucker –"

"Watch your mouth when you're talking to me. I am still your husband," said Alberto.

"Where you put your tiny cock would suggest otherwise."

"You can shut your goddamn mouth. Fucking dyke."

"It was the only way I could have a good orgasm," she said.

"I'd like to think you weren't always such a puta... but I remember how we met."

"Give me my money, Alberto. Give me my fucking MONEY!"

Dario sat in the chair in front of her, watching her cautiously, as her hand turned powder white as she gripped the phone so hard he wouldn't be surprised if she snapped it in half. She slammed the phone down on the receiver and she screamed. "That son of a bitch!"

Dario stayed unmoved. It was the first thing she noticed when she began to calm down. Most men would get antsy. God knows her children would scatter. Alberto would either get upset or excuse himself. But Dario sat there. Amid her rage. Unfazed. "He's robbing me..." she said.

"That's what it looks like." Dario stood up and walked around the desk and pulled her chair out for her. "Sit down..." he said warmly, softly.

She listened to him. He gripped her shoulders and began massaging them. "Whatever you want to do, I'm here for you."

"What I want to do..." She gripped his hands and squeezed them. Spinning around the chair, she looked up at him... "What I want to do is forget about him right now?"

"I can help you with that," said Dario. "I can help you with that easily." He bent forward and she tilted her head up to him and he kissed her lips. His mouth was sure and soft and his hand ran up her arms and to her breasts, as he slunk himself down to his knees between her legs. He ran his hands up her legs, the rough pads of his fingers scratching against her skin and feeling amazing as he found her underwear. She arched her body as he slid them down her legs. "You are the queen…" Dario said, before slipping his head between her thighs. His lips kissed her legs. The bristles of his beard felt great rubbing against her.

"I should kill him…" she said. "I should kill Alberto." Her head rocked back as Dario sealed his mouth over her sex. She closed her eyes. Giving herself over to the pleasure. To the experience. To his warm mouth and skilled tongue. "Yes," she said… "I should fucking kill him."

4)

"You want the world?" Griselda asked Pablo Escobar in his own little office that used to belong to Fabio Restrepo, before he put a bullet in his head. Pablo Escobar enjoyed a cigar and let out a cloud of smoke as he sat forward, interested. There was still a little stain of blood on the floor where Fabio Restrepo bled out. It was something that Griselda took notice of and was impressed by. Pablo probably kept it there as a reminder to others as much as himself, not to get too cocky and not to think that there's an escape at the end of this.

"I do, Madrina. I want the whole world," he said.

"You won't get there with one hundred kilos. You know that?"

"We all have to start somewhere."

"We do. I started in weed and making a few thousand dollars a week. I understand. But what if you could start a lot bigger and a lot faster?"

"I would like that a lot."

"You have routes into Miami. I have people from New York through the whole United States that I can bring to work for you in Miami. And we can build a network that feeds the entire country all the drugs it would ever want."

"How much?"

"You're not going to get world domination with five hundred kilos a year. But two thousand, three thousand… Five thousand, maybe even ten thousand kilos… well then you'll make more money than the Rockefellers. You'll be on Forbe's 500 List as one of the richest men in the world. You could do that. I could help you do that."

Pablo Escobar put out his cigar. His hands were flat on the table. An excitement ran through his body and he was waiting for the catch. Waiting for what he needed to do. Griselda waited for him to process it all. "And why would you want to help me?"

"Do you like Colombia?"

"I love it."

"I don't. The memories of these streets, for as beautiful as they are, are full of pain for me. My children love America too. They love Colombia, don't get me wrong. I've given them a good life here and everywhere. But America is where they want to be. Juan Ochoa needs a contact in Colombia, as he's making his own moves in getting cocaine through New York, and we need someone to work here in Colombia. You could be that person. You could manage the supply and we can take care a lot of the routes for you."

Pablo nods. "And what's the split?"

"We'll negotiate all of that later."

"What do I have to do? What do you want?"

Griselda smiled and crossed her legs. She knew she had him on the hook. She knew he would do just about anything for the power she had laid in front of him.

"Right now... I need a few of your men willing to get bloody if need be, willing to kill, and I need them to come with me tonight, no questions, and kill anyone that's a threat, and help me sever ties with a former business partner."

Pablo laughed. "That's all? You want some men? Some of my men? You can have as many as you need, La Madrina. I'll give you a fucking army if you want. Tell me where and when they need to be and they will be there for you."

Griselda nodded and uncrossed her legs and stood up. She stuck out her hand. "I think we'll have the start of a beneficial partnership."

5)

"Alberto," she said over the phone. "This isn't working. We need to talk and we need to talk in person."

"About what?"

"About business. About the money. About our fucking marriage," she snapped into the phone. "We need to talk about it all."

"Well, excuse me if I'm not sure that I want to come to the house I pay for. I think that's a good way for me never to leave that house again."

"Where do you want to meet?"

"There's a car lot, usually empty on the weekdays, near La Vida Noche We'll meet there. Tonight. At midnight. You come alone. Okay?"

"Fine Alberto... so scared of your wife, are you?"

"Fuck you Griselda."

"I'll see you then." She hung up the phone and looked at Dario. "I have a meeting."

"I'll have Pablo's men scope the place out and get in position. He won't see them coming," said Dario.

"Do that… But I'm going to that meeting."

"You could get hurt."

"I've been married to him for nearly six years. Though he wouldn't have much of what he had without me, I wouldn't have any of this without him. If he's going to die, I'm going to kill him. It's only right. He deserves that much," said Griselda.

"Never knew you to be a sentimentalist."

"I need to watch him die, Dario. I need him to know that the woman he forgot about, the woman he is treating like some dowry housewife, is the woman that was responsible for all of this… The woman capable of making all this happen. The woman that was ready to kill him and the woman that kills him."

"You look gorgeous when you're ready for vengeance."

"The kids are out of the house," she said.

Dario got up and shut the door to her office and began to unfasten his belt, while Griselda dropped her dress. Violence had a way of making her horny.

6)

Night in Medellin was one of the few things she liked more than New York. The sky was full of stars and the neighborhoods dark. Driving by herself through the midnight city, she saw the addicts, the hustlers, the people that were her people for so long.

When she pulled into the lot, there were a few cars parked in the lot. Alberto stood with men off in the corner, smoking a cigarette or a joint. She couldn't tell. She stopped her car and got out of it.

"Why are we here?" Alberto asked loudly. His men turned at attention. "Why did you want to see me?"

Griselda was sweating already, nervous, excited, a mix of emotions that wrapped around her and made her nervous. Wearing a plush shirt, her short, peppered hair was tied back with a hair tie. "Why did you bring so many men for a meeting, Alberto?"

"They're security." There were six men. Six men with handguns at the ready, waiting for something to happen.

"I'm your wife. Do you think I mean to kill you?"

"I think anything is possible."

"You're trying to cut me out of the business that I made."

"That you made?" Alberto scoffed. "You have a fucking ego. You stupid fucking cunt. You'd be sucking cock in a Medellin brothel if it wasn't for me. Taking it up the ass for any chulo with a few pesos. I was the one that ran the drug trade. You were the pathetic whore that was with an even more pathetic bitch of a man."

Griselda stayed calm. A pleasant expression filling her face. A look that made Alberto more nervous than if she was red with rage. "I was the one that saw the market for coke. I was the one that figured out the transport routes. I was the one that made any of this possible. Without me, you would've been dead and gone a long time ago. Or in prison. Because you were too fucking stupid to know how to avoid it. But I'm glad you said what you said," said Griselda.

"Oh, really...?" Alberto asked. "Why?"

"Because it makes this easier. Fuego!" she yelled. Suddenly gunfire crisscrossed the car park, coming from a small booth, from inside cars, from everywhere.

She yanked a gun from the back of her pants and took aim at Alberto. She pulled the trigger before Alberto could get his barring and fired the first shot into his chest as he got his Uzi free and pulled the trigger.

He went down hard on the ground, straight back, blood pushing from his mouth the moment his back hit the dirt. Pain shot through Griselda's stomach and Griselda gripped her abdomen and fell down to the ground. His men lay dead. Her men were getting out of the car to see their work. She knew she couldn't stop here, though. She had to make sure he was dead. There was no stopping now... He would know who she was.

She crawled over to a car parked near him. Each movement was like fire through her entire body. Pushing herself up on her knees, she grabbed hold of the trunk of the sky-blue Renault and got to her feet. She slid across the vehicle, walking to her husband, leaving a blood stain with every step.

The smell of gunpowder lingered in the air so thick that it stung the eyes. Men moaned in pain. Writhing on the ground, clenching bullet-ridden bodies and feeling the slow and brutal release of death coming for them. Griselda was standing, her hand pressed to her stomach, the warm feel of blood gushing through her fingers. Her body leaned against an old shot-to-hell sky-blue Renault 4. She really didn't want to die next to such a shitty vehicle.

This hadn't gone down exactly as she thought it would. None of this happened how she thought it would. She stared at her husband. Her soon to be deceased husband. Choking to death on his own blood, gasping mists of it covering his face. Watching him struggle, she felt a slight satisfaction. Even if this was going to be her last breath. Even if this was what did her in. Griselda knew she lived to be number one. She outlived Alberto. "You son of a bitch. I told you. I told you. I don't play second to anyone," Griselda shouted, dropping to her knees, and crawling herself the small distance to him. She picked up the Uzi he tried to unload on her. She ran her hands over his bloody face as his fading brown eyes looked in her direction. Even now, she still thought he was handsome. His thin face and narrow mustache. He could've been a movie star.

"We came so far, mi esposo... You just couldn't..." She winced from the pain in her stomach. "You just couldn't fucking respect all I did for you." She pulled the trigger and his head rocked and his face disappeared into a bloody mess.

Dario ran over to her, helping her to her feet. She had thought Alberto couldn't be trusted, and she was right. It was why she knew she needed Pablo's men. She took aim at the rest of her husband's men, those still moving, and ran the Uzi over all of them, until silence filled the small car park. "We must get you to the hospital, Madrina," said Dario. His hands were tender. His touch was delicate but urgent. She felt cared for again.

Draping her arm over his shoulder. He supported her.

Holding her, he grunted as he got her to her car. "You need a doctor."

She glared one last moment at Alberto Bravo, at the destruction, at the violence, trying to figure out how it all came to this as she closed her eyes in the backseat, and continued to feel blood push through her fingers. If she died... she died... it was worth it. She died the winner!

6)

Dario Sepulveda didn't leave her side. He stood in the hospital at the foot of her bed, after the doctor's spent hours making sure she didn't die. Others guarded the door with guns.

Her eyes opened.

She took a sour breath. "Madrina," Dario said immediately. "Alberto's dead."

Griselda Blanco sighed, shifting uncomfortably, listening to the beeping of her heart monitor, letting her know she was still alive. "And his men?" she whispered.

"All dead," said Dario.

"Any complaints?"

"Only that you didn't do it sooner, Madrina," said Sepulveda. "No one in the Ochoa family will miss him. They know who was making their money. No policias are bothering you either. They know that will be bad for their health. You recover Madrina... I will watch you."

"I appreciate it, Dario," she said. "I need you to make a couple of other calls for me."

"To who?"

"Forgers... I want to get passports and IDs for the both of us... I want to go to Miami."

"Will do Madrina."

"Dario…"

"Si?"

"Call me Griselda."

Dario looked at her. He thought he might just be in love with her. "Si, Griselda. Sleep… let me take care of everything. Let me take care of you."

Griselda shut her eyes, knowing she was the boss now. She did it. The world awaited her. Miami awaited her.

7)

"I've never seen someone so fucking miserable over getting 34 arrests, three hundred pounds of cocaine, pot, heroin… Operation Banshee will go down in history as one of the most successful operations ever done by a multi-department task force. It's gonna set the standard. You destroyed an entire drug operation," said Agent Shorn to Roberto.

Roberto stared at the folder with Griselda Blanco's name on it. His fingers tapping on it. "We didn't get who we were after. We disrupted stuff. But cocaine is still coming in. Pot is still pouring in. Heroin is still pouring in. If we don't get the distributors, then we have nothing. And we didn't get them. We don't even know who the fuck this Griselda Blanco is, or what she looks like."

"You really don't know how to take a win, know that? You're a real downer sometimes. It's probably why you don't have many friends."

Roberto smirked. "I don't have friends because most people are stupid and I'd rather not spend time with them."

"Yeah, I'm sure, it's the people that are the problem. Look… This is what we're going to do… you listening… you listening?" Shorn grabbed the folder from beneath Roberto's fingers and he walked over to the filing cabinet. "We're going to put this in a filing cabinet. You're going to come out with the rest of the guys from the task force. We're going to drink too much. You're going to take a cab home to your wife. And you're going to fuck her and not think about what didn't happen, and focus on what did."

"This is going to come back to bite us in the ass," said Roberto. "This was our chance to really put a hole in cocaine. Instead, they're celebrating that we got all that heroin off the street. They don't realize the insanity that is about to come. Cocaine went from nothing to one of the biggest drugs in five years. Where's it going to be in another five years? Where's it's going to be in fifteen? We could've stomped a hole in its popularity… but we missed it… We missed that window. And we're going to pay the price."

Shorn stared at him, amused, shaking his head, and laughing. "Can you tell me the lottery numbers tomorrow? I'll win and quit this fucking job."

"What?"

"If you're able to look into the future… I mean, why the hell not do it for something profitable?"

Roberto rolled his eyes. "We also may have created a monster," said Roberto.

"With what?"

"Fredrico Maslany… He made it possible, but he's been moving in on the territories, swooping up… and it's only going to be a matter of time –"

"Enough Rob… We'll catch them later. That's all we can do. So drinks." Shorn held the file over the filing cabinet, shaking it.

Roberto nodded, and Shorn dropped the file into the cabinet and shut it. He pushed himself off his chair and Shorn tossed an arm over his shoulder. "Let's try not to bum everyone out with your doom and gloom predictions."

"I'm right."

"You might be," said Shorn. "But there's nothing that we can do about it now."

He looked back at the filing cabinet and turned to the elevator. She'd pop some time. She would show her head sooner or later, and when she did… He'd be there to catch her.

MIKE ENEMIGO PRESENTS

THE CELL BLOCK
BOOK SUMMARIES

MIKE ENEMIGO is the new prison/street art sensation who has written and published several books. He is inspired by emotion; hope; pain; dreams and nightmares. He physically lives somewhere in a California prison cell where he works relentlessly creating his next piece. His mind and soul are elsewhere; seeing, studying, learning, and drawing inspiration to tear down suppressive walls and inspire the culture by pushing artistic boundaries.

THE CELL BLOCK is an independent multimedia company with the objective of accurately conveying the prison/street experience with the credibility and honesty that only one who has lived it can deliver, through literature and other arts, and to entertain and enlighten while doing so. Everything published by The Cell Block has been created by a prisoner, while in a prison cell.

THE BEST RESOURCE DIRECTORY FOR PRISONERS, $19.99 & $7.00 S/H: This book has over 1,450 resources for prisoners! Includes: Pen-Pal Companies! Non-Nude Photo Sellers! Free Books and Other Publications! Legal Assistance! Prisoner Advocates! Prisoner Assistants! Correspondence Education! Money-Making Opportunities! Resources for Prison Writers, Poets, Artists! And much, much more! Anything you can think of doing from your prison cell, this book contains the resources to do it!

A GUIDE TO RELAPSE PREVENTION FOR PRISONERS, $15.00 & $5.00 S/H: This book provides the information and guidance that can make a real difference in the preparation of a comprehensive relapse prevention plan. Discover how to meet the parole board's expectation using these proven and practical principles. Included is a blank template and sample relapse prevention plan to assist in your preparation.

LOST ANGELS: $15.00 & $5.00: David Rodrigo was a child who belonged to no world; rejected for his mixed heritage by most of his family and raised by an outcast uncle in the mean streets of East L.A. Chance cast him into a far darker and more devious pit of intrigue that stretched from the barest gutters to the halls of power in the great city. Now, to survive the clash of lethal forces arrayed about him, and to protect those he loves, he has only two allies; his quick wits, and the flashing blade that earned young David the street name, Viper.

LOYALTY AND BETRAYAL DELUXE EDITION, $19.99 & $7.00 S/H: Chunky was an associate of and soldier for the notorious Mexican Mafia – La Eme. That is, of course, until he was betrayed by those, he was most loyal to. Then he vowed to become their worst enemy. And though they've attempted to kill him numerous times, he still to this day is running around making a mockery of their organization .... This is the story of how it all began.

MONEY IZ THE MOTIVE: SPECIAL 2-IN-1 EDITION, $19.99 & $7.00 S/H: Like most kids growing up in the hood, Kano has a dream of going from rags to riches. But when his plan to get fast money by robbing the local "mom and pop" shop goes wrong, he quickly finds himself sentenced to serious prison time. Follow Kano as he is schooled to the ways of the game by some of the most respected OGs whoever did it; then is set free and given the resources to put his schooling into action and build the ultimate hood empire...

DEVILS & DEMONS: PART 1, $15.00 & $5.00 S/H: When Talton leaves the West Coast to set up shop in Florida he meets the female version of himself: A drug dealing murderess with psychological issues. A whirlwind of sex, money and murder inevitably ensues and Talton finds himself on the run from the law with nowhere to turn to. When his team from home finds out he's in trouble, they get on a plane heading south...

DEVILS & DEMONS: PART 2, $15.00 & $5.00 S/H: The Game is bitter-sweet for Talton, aka Gangsta. The same West Coast Clique who came to his aid ended up putting bullets into the chest of the woman he had fallen in love with. After leaving his ride or die in a puddle of her own blood, Talton finds himself on a flight back to Oak Park, the neighborhood where it all started...

DEVILS & DEMONS: PART 3, $15.00 & $5.00 S/H: Talton is on the road to retribution for the murder of the love of his life. Dante and his crew of killers are on a path of no return. This urban classic is based on real-life West Coast underworld politics. See what happens when a group of YG's find themselves in the midst of real underworld demons...

DEVILS & DEMONS: PART 4, $15.00 & $5.00 S/H: After waking up from a coma, Alize has locked herself away from the rest of the world. When her sister Brittany and their friend finally take her on a girl's night out, she meets Luck – a drug dealing womanizer.

FREAKY TALES, $15.00 & $5.00 S/H: *Freaky Tales* is the first book in a brand-new erotic series. King Guru, author of the *Devils & Demons* books, has put together a collection of sexy short stories and memoirs. In true TCB fashion, all of the erotic tales included in this book have been loosely based on true accounts told to, or experienced by the author.

THE ART & POWER OF LETTER WRITING FOR PRISONERS: DELUXE EDITION $19.99 & $7.00 S/H: When locked inside a prison cell, being able to write well is the most powerful skill you can have! Learn how to increase your power by writing high-quality personal and formal letters! Includes letter templates, pen-pal website strategies, punctuation guide and more!

THE PRISON MANUAL: $19.99 & $7.00 S/H: *The Prison Manual* is your all-in-one book on how to not only survive the rough terrain of the American prison system, but use it to your advantage so you can THRIVE from it! How to Use Your Prison Time to YOUR Advantage; How to Write Letters that Will Give You Maximum Effectiveness; Workout and Physical Health Secrets that Will Keep You as FIT as Possible; The Psychological impact of incarceration and How to Maintain Your MAXIMUM Level of Mental Health; Prison Art Techniques; Fulfilling Food Recipes; Parole Preparation Strategies and much, MUCH more!

GET OUT, STAY OUT!, $16.95 & $5.00 S/H: This book should be in the hands of everyone in a prison cell. It reveals a challenging but clear course for overcoming the obstacles that stand between prisoners and their freedom. For those behind bars, one goal outshines all others: GETTING OUT! After being released, that goal then shifts to STAYING OUT! This book will help prisoners do both. It has been masterfully constructed into five parts that will help prisoners maximize focus while they strive to accomplish whichever goal is at hand.

MOB$TAR MONEY, $12.00 & $4.00 S/H: After Trey's mother is sent to prison for 75 years to life, he and his little brother are moved from their home in Sacramento,

California, to his grandmother's house in Stockton, California where he is forced to find his way in life and become a man on his own in the city's grimy streets. One day, on his way home from the local corner store, Trey has a rough encounter with the neighborhood bully. Luckily, that's when Tyson, a member of the MOBTAR, a local "get money" gang comes to his aid. The two kids quickly become friends, and it doesn't take long before Trey is embraced into the notorious MOB$TAR money gang, which opens the door to an adventure full of sex, money, murder and mayhem that will change his life forever... You will never guess how this story ends!

BLOCK MONEY, $12.00 & $4.00 S/H: Beast, a young thug from the grimy streets of central Stockton, California lives The Block; breathes The Block; and has committed himself to bleed The Block for all it's worth until his very last breath. Then, one day, he meets Nadia; a stripper at the local club who piques his curiosity with her beauty, quick-witted intellect and rider qualities. The problem? She has a man – Esco – a local kingpin with money and power. It doesn't take long, however, before a devious plot is hatched to pull off a heist worth an indeterminable amount of money. Following the acts of treachery, deception and betrayal are twists and turns and a bloody war that will leave you speechless!

HOW TO HUSTLE AND WIN: SEX, MONEY, MURDER EDITION $15.00 & $5.00 S/H: *How To Hu$tle and Win: Sex, Money, Murder Edition* is the grittiest, underground self-help manual for the 21st century street entrepreneur in print. Never has there been such a book written for today's gangsters, goons and go-getters. This self-help handbook is an absolute must-have for anyone who is actively connected to the streets.

RAW LAW: YOUR RIGHTS, & HOW TO SUE WHEN THEY ARE VIOLATED! $15.00 & $5.00 S/H:

Raw Law For Prisoners is a clear and concise guide for prisoners and their advocates to understanding civil rights laws guaranteed to prisoners under the US Constitution, and how to successfully file a lawsuit when those rights have been violated! From initial complaint to trial, this book will take you through the entire process, step by step, in simple, easy-to-understand terms. Also included are several examples where prisoners have sued prison officials successfully, resulting in changes of unjust rules and regulations and recourse for rights violations, oftentimes resulting in rewards of thousands, even millions of dollars in damages! If you feel your rights have been violated, don't lash out at guards, which is usually ineffective and only makes matters worse. Instead, defend yourself successfully by using the legal system, and getting the power of the courts on your side!

HOW TO WRITE URBAN BOOKS FOR MONEY & FAME: $16.95 & $5.00 S/H: Inside this book you will learn the true story of how Mike Enemigo and King Guru have received money and fame from inside their prison cells by writing urban books; the secrets to writing hood classics so you, too, can be caked up and famous; proper punctuation using hood examples; and resources you can use to achieve your money motivated ambitions! If you're a prisoner who want to write urban novels for money and fame, this must-have manual will give you all the game!

PRETTY GIRLS LOVE BAD BOYS: AN INMATE'S GUIDE TO GETTING GIRLS: $15.00 & $5.00 S/H: Tired of the same, boring, cliché pen pal books that don't tell you what you really need to know? If so, this book is for you! Anything you need to know on the art of long and short distance seduction is included within these pages! Not only does it give you the science of attracting pen pals from websites, it also includes psychological profiles and instructions on how to seduce any woman you set your sights on! Includes interviews of women who have fallen in love with prisoners, bios for pen pal ads, pre-written love letters, romantic poems, love-song lyrics, jokes and much, much more! This book is the ultimate guide – a must-have for any prisoner who refuses to let prison walls affect their MAC'n.

THE LADIES WHO LOVE PRISONERS, $15.00 & $5.00 S/H: New Special Report reveals the secrets of real women who have fallen in love with prisoners, regardless of crime, sentence, or location. This info will give you a HUGE advantage in getting girls from prison.

THE MILLIONAIRE PRISONER: PART 1, $16.95 & $5.00 S/H

THE MILLIONAIRE PRISONER: PART 2, $16.95 & $5.00 S/H

THE MILLIONAIRE PRISONER: SPECIAL 2-IN-1 EDITION, $24.99 & $7.00 S/H: Why wait until you get out of prison to achieve your dreams? Here's a blueprint that you can use to become successful! *The Millionaire Prisoner* is your complete reference to overcoming any obstacle in prison. You won't be able to put it down! With this book you will discover the secrets to: Making money from your cell! Obtain FREE money for correspondence courses! Become an expert on any topic! Develop the habits of the rich! Network with celebrities! Set up your own website! Market your products, ideas and services! Successfully use prison pen pal websites! All of this and much, much more! This book has enabled thousands of prisoners to succeed and it will show you the way also!

THE MILLIONAIRE PRISONER 3: SUCCESS UNIVERSITY, $16.95 & $5.00 S/H: Why wait until you get out of prison to achieve your dreams? Here's a new-look blueprint that you can use to be successful! *The Millionaire*

Prisoner 3 contains advanced strategies to overcoming any obstacle in prison. You won't be able to put it down!

THE MILLIONAIRE PRISONER 4: PEN PAL MASTERY, $16.95 & $5.00 S/H: Tired of subpar results? Here's a master blueprint that you can use to get tons of pen pals! *TMP 4: Pen Pal Mastery* is your complete roadmap to finding your one true love. You won't be able to put it down! With this book you'll DISCOVER the SECRETS to: Get FREE pen pals & which sites are best to use; successful tactics female prisoners can win with; use astrology to find love, friendship & more, build a winning social media presence. All of this and much more!

THE MILLIONAIRE PRISONER 5: FREE MONEY, $24.95 & $7.00 S/H: Wish you could find more FREE MONEY like your stimulus? Seeking an end to your money problems? Look no further! Here's a master blueprint that reveals all that's available! *Tmp 5: Free Money* is your complete roadmap to finding all the FREE MONEY options out there for convicts. You won't be able to put it down!

GET OUT, GET RICH: HOW TO GET PAID LEGALLY WHEN YOU GET OUT OF PRISON!, $16.95 & $5.00 S/H: Many of you are incarcerated for a money-motivated crime. But w/ today's tech & opportunities, not only is the crime-for-money risk/reward ratio not strategically wise, it's not even necessary. You can earn much more money by partaking in any one of the easy, legal hustles explained in this book, regardless of your record. Help yourself earn an honest income so you can not only make a lot of money, but say good-bye to penitentiary chances and prison forever! (Note: Many things in this book can even he done from inside prison.) (ALSO PUBLISHED AS *HOOD MILLIONAIRE: HOW TO HUSTLE AND WIN LEGALLY!*)

THE CEO MANUAL: HOW TO START A BUSINESS WHEN YOU GET OUT OF PRISON, $16.95 & $5.00 S/H: $16.95 & $5.00 S/H: This new book will teach you the simplest way to start your own business when you get out of prison. Includes: Start-up Steps! The Secrets to Pulling Money from Investors! How to Manage People Effectively! How To Legally Protect Your Assets from "them"! Hundreds of resources to get you started, including a list of "loan friendly" banks! (ALSO PUBLISHED AS *CEO MANUAL: START A BUSINESS, BE A BOSS!*)

THE MONEY MANUAL: UNDERGROUND CASH SECRETS EXPOSED! 16.95 & $5.00 S/H: Becoming a millionaire is equal parts what you make, and what you don't spend – AKA save. All Millionaires and Billionaires have mastered the art of not only making money, but keeping the money they make (remember Donald Trump's tax maneuvers?), as well as establishing credit so that they are loaned money by banks and trusted with money from investors: AKA OPM – other people's money. And did you know there are millionaires and billionaires just waiting to GIVE money away? It's true! These are all very-little known secrets "they" don't want YOU to know about, but that I'm exposing in my new book!

HOOD MILLIONAIRE; HOW TO HUSTLE & WIN LEGALLY, $16.95 & $5.00 S/H: Hustlin' is a way of life in the hood. We all have money motivated ambitions, not only because we gotta eat, but because status is oftentimes determined by one's own salary. To achieve what we consider financial success, we often invest our efforts into illicit activities – we take penitentiary chances. This leads to a life in and out of prison, sometimes death – both of which are counterproductive to gettin' money. But there's a solution to this, and I have it...

CEO MANUAL: START A BUSINESS BE A BOSS, $16.95 & $5.00 S/H: After the success of the urban-entrepreneur classic *Hood Millionaire: How To Hustle & Win Legally!*, self-made millionaires Mike Enemigo and Sav Hustle team back up to bring you the latest edition of the Hood Millionaire series – *CEO Manual: Start A Business, Be A Boss!* In this latest collection of game laying down the art of "hoodpreneurship", you will learn such things as: 5 Core Steps to Starting Your Own Business! 5 Common Launch Errors You Must Avoid! How To Write a Business Plan! How To Legally Protect Your Assets From "Them"! How To Make Your Business Fundable, Where to Get Money for Your Start-up Business, and even How to Start a Business With No Money! You will learn How to Drive Customers to Your Website, How to Maximize Marketing Dollars, Contract Secrets for the savvy boss, and much, much more! And as an added bonus, we have included over 200 Business Resources, from government agencies and small business development centers, to a secret list of small-business friendly banks that will help you get started!

PAID IN FULL: WELCOME TO DA GAME, $15.00 & $5.00 S/H. In 1983, the movie *Scarface* inspired many kids growing up in America's inner cities to turn their rags into riches by becoming cocaine kingpins. Harlem's Azie Faison was one of them. Faison would ultimately connect with Harlem's Rich Porter and Alpo Martinez, and the trio would go on to become certified street legends of the '80s and early '90s. Years later, Dame Dash and Roc-A-Fella Films would tell their story in the based-on-actual-events movie, *Paid in Full*.

But now, we are telling the story our way – The Cell Block way – where you will get a perspective of the story that the movie did not show, ultimately learning an outcome that you did not expect.

Book one of our series, *Paid in Full: Welcome to da Game*, will give you an inside look at a key player in this story, one that is not often talked about – Lulu, the

Columbian cocaine kingpin with direct ties to Pablo Escobar, who plugged Azie in with an unlimited amount of top-tier cocaine at dirt-cheap prices that helped boost the trio to neighborhood superstars and certified kingpin status... until greed, betrayal, and murder destroyed everything....(ALSO PUBLISHED AS *CITY OF GODS*.)

OJ'S LIFE BEHIND BARS, $15.00 & $5 S/H: In 1994, Heisman Trophy winner and NFL superstar OJ Simpson was arrested for the brutal murder of his ex-wife Nicole Brown-Simpson and her friend Ron Goldman. In 1995, after the "trial of the century," he was acquitted of both murders, though most of the world believes he did it. In 2007 OJ was again arrested, but this time in Las Vegas, for armed robbery and kidnapping. On October 3, 2008 he was found guilty sentenced to 33 years and was sent to Lovelock Correctional Facility, in Lovelock, Nevada. There he met inmate-author Vernon Nelson. Vernon was granted a true, insider's perspective into the mind and life of one of the country's most notorious men; one that has never been provided...until now.

THE MOB, $16.99 & $5.00 S/H: PaperBoy is a Bay Area boss who has invested blood, sweat, and years into building The Mob – a network of Bay Area street legends, block bleeders, and underground rappers who collaborate nationwide in the interest of pushing a multi-million-dollar criminal enterprise of sex, drugs, and murder.

Based on actual events, little has been known about PaperBoy, the mastermind behind The Mob, and intricate details of its operation, until now.

Follow this story to learn about some of the Bay Area underworld's most glamorous figures and famous events...

MOB TALES, $16.95 & $5.00 S/H. In 1992, Suge 'The Mobfather' Knight launched Death Row Records with a rumored 1.5-million-dollar investment from then-incarcerated drug kingpin Michael 'Harry O' Harris. Under Suge

Knight's leadership, Death Row would go on to boast a roster consisting of some of the greatest names in hip-hop history, such as Dr. Dre, Snoop Dogg, and Tupac Shakur. Suge ultimately generated well over 200 million dollars selling records that detailed life in the streets.

Now, from his prison cell, Suge Knight has partnered up with incarcerated publishing boss Mike Enemigo, and longtime Mob affiliate O.G. Silk, to create Death Row Publishing, and drop a new series, *Mob Tales*, as a platform to shed light on some of the hottest incarcerated street-lit authors in the game today. Each book in this series will be a collection of stories written by those who have lived that of which they write, and who are surely to be among the next generation of street-lit legends.

COCAINE QUEEN, $17.95 & $5.00 S/H. She was a loving mother.
She was also a ruthless and treacherous drug lord who's suspected of murdering more than one husband.

Who was she?

Griselda Blanco, the Queen of Cocaine, aka The Godmother.

From the streets of New York, to the ghettoes of Columbia, to the mansions of Miami, *Cocaine Queen: The Reign of Griselda Blanco*, is a based-on-actual-events story that takes you on a dangerous ride along the bloody rise to power of the most notorious female drug lord in history, as she kills anyone who gets in her way of complete dominance of the American cocaine market....

COCAINE QUEEN 2, $17.95 & $5.00 S/H. She was a loving mother.
She was also a ruthless and treacherous drug lord who's suspected of murdering more than one husband.

Who was she?

Griselda Blanco, the Queen of Cocaine, aka The Godmother.

From the streets of New York, to the ghettoes of Columbia, to the mansions of Miami, *Cocaine Queen: The Reign of Griselda Blanco*, is a based-on-actual-events story that takes you on a dangerous ride along the bloody rise to power of the most notorious female drug lord in history, as she kills anyone who gets in her way of complete dominance of the American cocaine market....

SOSA: THE PRICE OF POWER (BOOK ONE), $19.95 & $5.00 S/H: The 1983 classic gangster film *Scarface wooed* over a billion fans worldwide, but it ended in the abrupt, violent massacre of Tony and his squad at the behest of ruthless Bolivian crime boss, Alejandro Sosa.

Since then, *Scarface* has birthed a nation of diehards who have been waiting decades for a Hollywood response. The wait is now over. Tony is dead, but his legacy lives inside of Elvira, who has resurfaced in the riveting masterpiece saga entitled: *Sosa; The Price of Power*. First, Sosa must scramble to pick up the pieces which were left shattered by the betrayal of Tony.

The true *Scarface* fan will be glued to the coldblooded cunning, the bigger-than-life characters who Sosa surrounds himself with, and the skilled moves he makes on an international scale. For the blonde bombshell, the game becomes life or death. Who can't remember Tony's enemies: Gaspar Gomez, the Diaz brothers and others? They are the Miami Cuban Mafia and are hunting Elvira down for the huge nine-figure fortune her husband left behind....

SOSA: THE REIGN (BOOK TWO), $19.95 & $5.00 S/H: In book one of this mega-hit series, *Sosa: The Price of Power*, Elvira appealed to Sosa to protect her from the Miami Cuban Mafia (MCM), who were trying to force her to hand over millions of dollars left by her dead husband. Surprised but eager, Sosa sent a couple of his best assassins to Miami to neutralize the MCM and muscle them into backing off the pregnant bombshell. Now Elvira (who may or may not know Sosa had Tony Montana hit) has made a new ally and friend, but with her husband out of the picture, Sosa finds himself in need of a solid business contact inside of the USA.

With Dr. Orlando Gutierrez assassinated, Sosa and his powerful crime syndicate literally has brand-new life and partners: The CIA. Sosa was expressly requested by the Americans to assist them with helping the Nicaraguan Contra Army stay afloat in the fight against the Sandinista Government. In return, Sosa demands that U.S. Marine Colonel Oliver North allow his organization – La Corporacion Mafia Cruenza – be allowed to fly fifty jets several times per week into the United States.

While Sosa, his Mafia, the CIA and President Ronald Reagan's National Security Advisor were involved in one of the most blatant and unethical conspiracies in American history, Elvira focuses on her pregnancy... and learns what real power feels like. As she absorbs that feeling, she learns also that she can't outrun demons buried in her past. To deal with them, she writes a book entitled *Dark Flight*.

It was a can of worms best kept closed....

AOB, $15.00 & $5.00 S/H. Growing up in the Bay Area, Manny Fresh the Best had a front-row seat to some of the coldest players to ever do it. And you already know, A.O.B. is the name of the Game! So, When Manny Fresh slides through Stockton one day and sees Rosa, a stupid-bad Mexican chick with a whole lotta 'talent' behind her walking down the street tryna get some money, he knew immediately what he had to do: Put it In My Pocket!

AOB 2, $15.00 & $5.00 S/H.

AOB 3, $15.00 & $5.00 S/H.

PIMPOLOGY: THE 7 ISMS OF THE GAME, $15.00 & $5.00 S/H: It's been said that if you knew better, you'd do better. So, in the spirit of dropping jewels upon the rare few who truly want to know how to win, this collection of exclusive Game has been compiled. And though a lot of so-called players claim to know how the Pimp Game is supposed to go, none have revealed the real. . . Until now!

JAILHOUSE PUBLISHING FOR MONEY, POWER & FAME: $19.99 & $7.00 S/H: In 2010, after flirting with the idea for two years, Mike Enemigo started writing his first book. In 2014, he officially launched his publishing company, The Cell Block, with the release of five books. Of course, with no mentor(s), how-to guides, or any real resources, he was met with failure after failure as he tried to navigate the treacherous goal of publishing books from his prison cell. However, he was determined to make it. He was determined to figure it out and he refused to quit. In Mike's new book, *Jailhouse Publishing for Money, Power, and Fame*, he breaks down all his jailhouse publishing secrets and strategies, so you can do all he's done, but without the trials and tribulations he's had to go through...

All books are available on thecellblock.net website.

You can also order by sending a money order or institutional check to:

The Cell Block
PO Box 1025
Rancho Cordova, CA 95741

www.ingramcontent.com/pod-product-compliance
Lightning Source LLC
Chambersburg PA
CBHW071428260626
47170CB00008B/2629

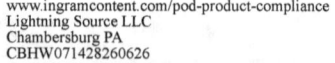